"Cheeky prose, delicious innuendo and wit, the clever juxtaposition of characters and a preposterous hero result in great entertainment."

—*Library Journal*

"Just as much fun as his first book . . . Dean has a way of poking fun at all the English country house conventions while constructing a true mystery, and the reader has fun right along with him. Give yourself a treat with *Faked to Death*."

—Charlaine Harris, author of *Club Dead*

"A perfect accompaniment to a rocking chair, a shady porch, and iced tea with mint."

—*The Houston Voice*

"The fun continues."

—*Publishers Weekly*

And more outstanding praise for Dean James and *Posted to Death*

"A delightful English village whodunit filled with some of the most eccentric characters you'll ever run across in a mystery novel."

—*The Denver Post*

"A worthy and cozy village mystery you can really sink your teeth into."

—*The Houston Chronicle*

"A wickedly funny send-up of the classic cozy British mystery. Dame Agatha would be rolling in her grave, unless she's already out of it."

—Nancy Pickard

"Agatha Award–winning author Dean James has penned a chatty charmer of a first book in this new cozy-with-a-kink series. *Posted to Death* will appeal especially to those who enjoy their murders mixed with mirth."

—*I Love a Mystery*

"A delight from start to finish. Everything you could wish for in a British cozy. Simon Kirby-Jones is a charming and intriguing sleuth who puts the village of Snupperton-Mumsley squarely on the mystery map."

—Dorothy Cannell

"Sure to revolutionize the traditional British cozy and win the hearts of fans everywhere . . . Quirky villagers, quaint cottages and an intriguing mystery told in the voice of a highly unusual protagonist with a rapier wit combine for a delightful reading experience."

—*Publishers Weekly (starred review)*

Books by Dean James

POSTED TO DEATH

FAKED TO DEATH

DECORATED TO DEATH

Published by Kensington Publishing Corporation

A Simon Kirby-Jones Mystery

FAKED TO DEATH

Dean James

KENSINGTON BOOKS
Kensington Publishing Corp.
http://www.kensingtonbooks.com

For Tejas
D.E.
T.F.A.

Acknowledgments

The year during which this book was written was both the worst and best of my life, and mere thanks aren't enough to express my appreciation for my family and friends for doing their best to see me through it. I couldn't have done it without you.

Beyond that, several people deserve special mention. Thanks to my editor, John Scognamiglio, for his continued enthusiasm for Simon and his adventures; to my agent, Nancy Yost, for being on my team and who is, thankfully, nothing at all like the agent in this book; and, finally, to Megan Bladen-Blinkoff, Julie Wray Herman, and Patricia Orr, who with unfailing good humor continue to offer support and constructive criticism, no matter how busy they are with their own lives and work.

Chapter One

Being dead has its advantages.

I get much more writing done now that I'm a vampire. When one has not one but two yearly best-sellers to produce, it's just as well that three hours' rest per night is sufficient.

The world of popular fiction knows me as Daphne Deepwood (historical romance) and Dorinda Darlington (hard-boiled female private eye novels). Little do my devoted readers suspect that Daphne-Dorinda is really Simon Kirby-Jones, respected historian, author of acclaimed biographies of Eleanor of Aquitaine and Richard the Lionheart. Nor do they suspect I'm a vampire. And gay.

Enough of *True Confessions*. It was writing that got me into this messy business in the first place. A couple of months after that unpleasantness over our murdered postmistress,[*] I was browsing innocently in The Book Chase, my local bookshop, when it all began.

A rustle of movement from the door intruded on my consciousness. I looked up from a shelf of mystery novels to see a tall twin set bedecked with pearls sailing my way.

"Dr. Kirby-Jones, I presume?"

Something rattled; it might have been the windows. I took a step back, but the twin set kept advancing.

"I'm afraid you have the advantage, ma'am," I told her, my back up against the mystery section.

"Not to worry," she assured me, looking down at me. She had an inch on me, and I'm a bit over six feet myself. "No need for all that fancy protocol. I'll just introduce myself." She stuck out a meaty paw at me, and I took it, amazed to find that her hand was bigger than mine. "Lady Hermione Kinsale, and very pleased to meet you. Read your work on Eleanor. Quite splendid, I must say."

Even though my eardrums were now tender— she had no idea that vampires have exquisitely sensitive hearing—I suppressed any notions of pain for the pleasure of a compliment, no matter how forcefully delivered.

I wiggled my fingers, relieved nothing had broken. With her height and matching build, she could probably toss me over her shoulder without blinking. I looked at her closely. Someone with her strength could be a vampire. But I didn't think she was. I'm learning to recognize others of my kind. Just tough as the proverbial old boot, our Lady Hermione.

---

[*] Kindly consult *Posted to Death* for further details.

Sixty if she was a day, but likely to last another forty years or so.

"Thank you, Lady Hermione. It's always gratifying to be recognized for one's work." Surely that sounded professorial enough to fit the image.

"You're just the man I'm looking for," Lady Hermione boomed at me. Alarmed, I glanced over at Trevor Chase, proprietor of the bookshop, and he winked broadly behind Lady Hermione's back. "Had a chap bow out on me for next week, and I need someone with your skills to fill in for him. Heard you were living in the area now, but I didn't expect to run into you so soon."

Trevor was grinning, and I was totally at sea.

"Writers' Week at Kinsale House: surely you've heard of them?" Lady Hermione didn't pause for a response. "Well known, they are, and you'd be an asset. The topic for next week's conference is the crime novel, and we need someone with your credentials to speak on historical mysteries. You'll be just the ticket." She turned and headed for the door. "See you for tea on Thursday afternoon at Kinsale House, and I'll explain what you're to do." The door shut firmly behind her, and the building seemed to breathe with relief.

After spending a few moments with Lady Hermione, one quite sees how the British amassed the world's largest empire.

Trevor burst out laughing. "Oh, Simon, my dear fellow, if only you could see your face."

"What *was* that?" I glared at him.

"Lady Hermione Kinsale, only surviving offspring of the eighth earl of Mumsley, and patroness of the arts. In this case, of writers." Trevor paused to relight his pipe. "A bit eccentric, but well meaning."

He puffed a fragrant cloud of smoke into the air, and I sniffed appreciatively.

"And now I'm simply supposed to *appear* at her writers' thingy?" My tone was indignant, but in truth, my little middle-class American self was tickled by the notion of spending time with the daughter of an earl. Even vampires can be snobs.

"I've no doubt you'll manage to enjoy yourself," Trevor assured me. "After all, what could happen at a writers' conference?"

I should have realized that Trevor had no gift for prophecy. Had I but known! Instead, I chatted with him for a few minutes longer, handed him a stack of books to ring up, then went merrily on my way back down the high street of Snupperton Mumsley to Laurel Cottage, my home of the past several months.

Inside, I carefully put away my hat, gloves, and sunglasses (even though I can go out during the day thanks to some special medication, it doesn't hurt to protect oneself as one can), then went into my office. Giles Blitherington, my handsome young secretary (or Executive Assistant, as he now labeled himself), called out from his smaller office next to mine, "Simon, did Trevor have that new book on the Anglo-Saxon church that I wanted?"

Putting the stack of books I'd brought home down on top of a pile of papers, I sat down behind my desk. "Yes, Giles, he did."

I glanced up as Giles appeared in the doorway. I picked up the book he wanted and held it out to him. He advanced toward me and reached for the book. His deep-blue eyes glowed with pleasure as he grasped it. I do like a man who gets excited over a book!

Not to mention the fact that Giles is also devilishly attractive. He doesn't know it, but he's the model for the hero in Daphne Deepwood's next masterpiece of historical fiction. That auburn hair and hunky build of his are perfect for a romance novel hero, but unlike Giles, my fictional Athelstan likes women. I much prefer the original the way he is, though it wouldn't do for him to know that.

"So what's new with Trevor?" Giles said, settling into the chair opposite my desk. He ran his hands back and forth over the book. He was dying to dig into it to find the material I needed for the current book, but he couldn't resist the opportunity for a quick gossip. "Still head over heels with his young mechanic?"

I frowned severely. "I can't imagine why you'd think that I'd ask Trevor any such thing." Giles laughed, because he knew me much better than that. I grinned. "Yes, he professes to be quite happy with the young man's handiwork. But I have something far more interesting to tell you!" Quickly I related my encounter with Lady Hermione Kinsale.

Giles whistled. "Simon, what a coup! My mother will be positively eaten up with jealousy. She has been trying for years to get Lady Hermione to notice her, but Mummy simply isn't arty enough for her." Lady Prunella Blitherington, Giles's mother, is more of a snob than I would ever dare to be, and her reaction to the news that Giles was going to work for me occasioned quite a little scene.** Since then, she and I have managed to get along quite well, as long as we stay out of each other's way. I chuckled at the thought of her reaction to this news. If I'd needed any further inducement to accede to Lady Hermione's royal command, this was it.

** Once again, kindly consult *Posted to Death*.

"Why, Sir Giles," I drawled, using his title, which normally he avoided, "I had no idea, when I first came to Snupperton Mumsley, that I'd be moving in such exalted circles. You'll have to tell me all about how to behave around the daughter of an earl so I don't embarrass myself."

"Just be your usual elegant, witty, and debonair self, Simon, and you won't have a single problem." Giles winked at me as he stood up. I waved him back to his office to work.

I actually employ him because he's very good at keeping me organized and helping me with my research, but the fact that he's charming is a distinct plus. Humming happily to myself, I settled in to work.

Two days later, standing at the impressive front door of Kinsale House, I recalled Trevor's assurance: *"What could happen?" Indeed!* I said to myself as I lifted the heavy, ornate knocker. Kinsale House was a monstrous pile, a mishmash of Georgian refinement and Victorian Gothic excess that would give an architectural historian nightmares. Obviously one or more previous earls of Mumsley had had more money than taste.

I banged the knocker against the massive oaken door for the second time. Almost at once the door slid open, and before me stood a man I presumed was the butler. He wore the proper attire, but the ring in his septum and the spiky bleached-blond hair were not quite what I had expected. He had the face of a moody pop star and the build of a footballer. I had the sudden notion that he might feature in an upcoming novel of mine.

"Good day, sir." He waved me in. His voice was

rich and well modulated. He looked barely thirty, but he had the manner of a man twice his age. "You must be Dr. Kirby-Jones. Lady Hermione awaits you in the morning room, where tea is being served."

"Yes, thank you," I said, following him. "And you are . . ."

"Dingleby, sir." He flashed a brief smile over his shoulder. Oh, yes, most interesting.

"Ah, Dingleby, thank you," Lady Hermione trumpeted when she caught sight of us. "Do come in, Dr. Kirby-Jones. You are most delightfully prompt."

I had stuffed my ears with cotton wool before leaving Laurel Cottage, and Lady Hermione's voice was now muted to an acceptable level.

Lady Hermione patted a spot beside her, and I tried to make myself comfortable on the hideously overstuffed Victorian sofa. Next to Lady Hermione, occupying a similarly frightful matching chair, perched a mousy woman with the large, frightened eyes of a rabbit facing a deadly snake. She watched me nervously, as if I were about to swoop across Lady Hermione and ravish her on the spot. Lady Hermione waved negligently in her direction. "My companion and secretary, Mary Monkley."

Mary nodded tentatively. "How do you do, Dr. Kirby-Jones?" Her voice came out in a whisper. I had to focus closely to be able to hear her. Perhaps prolonged exposure to Lady Hermione's loud voice and bombastic manner had so unnerved her that she responded to everyone like this. I could sympathize.

Lady Hermione shoved a cup of tea at me, and I did my best to keep the tea from sloshing onto my trousers. *Drat!* I held the cup and saucer in one hand while I dug in a pocket for a handkerchief with the other. As I was mopping up the tea from my lap, Lady Hermione, to whom a soggy lap was apparently of little consequence, proffered a plate of biscuits. I muttered a "No, thank you" as politely as I could, and Lady Hermione dropped the plate onto the table. As the plate hit with a loud *thunk*, Mary Monkley jerked as if she had been struck. I was surprised the plate hadn't shattered on impact.

"Now, to business," Lady Hermione said. "Doubtless you are well acquainted with the Writers' Week at Kinsale House." She actually paused for a brief moment before sweeping on. Giles had filled me in on the pertinent details. Lady Hermione had quite a good reputation for her writers' conferences, but I wondered how many of the attendees needed to take a cure for their shattered nerves by the end of the week. "It's quite fortunate that you live nearby, Dr. Kirby-Jones. We'll put you on the list of permanent speakers."

Lady Hermione beamed at me while I struggled to reply to this signal honor through a mouthful of tea. "You may thank me later, Dr. Kirby-Jones. As for next week's conference, as I told you, the theme is the crime novel, and we very much need someone with your expertise to speak on researching and writing the historical crime novel." She stuck out a hand toward Mary Monkley, and that hapless creature gave her several pieces of paper. Lady Hermione glanced over them, nodded approvingly, then gave them to me.

"Here's a schedule of the week's events, plus a list of our attendees. Your list of topics and assignments for one-on-one critiques is there, too. Before you go, Mary will give you the manuscripts you are to read." She actually paused for a breath, but before I could marshal my thoughts to reply, she swept on. "As you'll see, it's a small but select group. Intensive instruction and discussion—that's our hallmark."

She went on in the same vein, but I was no longer paying close attention. I had glanced down at the list of attendees and was thunderstruck at the inclusion of one name. According to the list, Dorinda Darlington was one of the week's featured authors.

Maybe Lady Hermione had dug up my deeply guarded secret, which I doubted.

Or maybe an impostor was trying to take advantage of my anonymity.

Chapter Two

Some agents might as well be vampires—of the old bloodsucking variety, that is. Others, like my English agent, Nina Yaknova, are pit bulls, although with her designer suits, elegant coiffures, and incandescent smile, Nina looks more like a cover girl for *Vogue* than the ruthless "best in show" scrapper she really is.

The morning after tea at Kinsale House, I caught a morning train from nearby Bedford up to London and arrived at Nina's office in Bloomsbury at the unfashionably early hour of nine. Nina's assistant took one look at my face and quelled his habitual rude greeting and instead motioned me straight into Nina's office. I was in no mood to put up with the boy toy's jealousy. If he had even an ounce of brains, he would have figured out by now that I'm not in the least interested in Nina as a potential bed partner. But Nina didn't hire him for the size of his brain.

"Sometimes, Simon," Nina said, her lip curling in annoyance as she beheld me in her doorway, "you're simply too, too American."

"I know I'm early, Nina, darling," I drawled as I seated myself in the ugly modern (read *uncomfortable*) chair Nina keeps for visiting clients. She doesn't like anyone to stay too long; it interferes with her work.

This was only the third time I had met with Nina face-to-face. My American agents had arranged for her to handle my work in the United Kingdom, assuring me that she had a solid reputation for developing her clients' careers and getting them consistently favorable contracts. The list of Nina's clients had impressed me, and among the list were a number of the top popular fiction writers. I was delighted to be included in so distinguished a list, though Nina sometimes disconcerted me with her manner of doing business.

Her phone burbled, and Nina frowned at me. She picked up the phone and listened for a moment, then said, her voice extravagant with patience, "Yes, Freddy, tell Ms. Harper that I'm in conference and cannot be interrupted. Like I've told you before. She'll understand."

She replaced the receiver in its cradle and threw me a look. "Not a word, Simon." She picked up a bundle of papers from her desk and made a show of stacking them in front of her. "Now, did you read that manuscript I sent you?"

"In a moment, Nina. I've something more important to discuss with you."

"Such drama, Simon. What on earth is the matter?" She leaned back in her chair and regarded me with ill-concealed amusement.

"I'll come right to the point, Nina," I said, already used to her little tactics. "Someone is impersonating me. Or, rather, impersonating Dorinda Darlington. What should we do about it?"

Nina didn't appear in the least surprised at my statement, which in turn really didn't surprise me. Nina likes her clients to think she's omniscient. "Nothing, at the moment."

"You don't seem all that surprised," I said, unnecessarily.

One hand, sporting an expensive diamond-and-emerald ring, waved my comment away. "I've already seen the program for the week at Kinsale House, Simon. I'm well aware of who's going to be there."

"I should have known," I said, chagrined. "I had forgotten that Isabella Veryan, George Austen-Hare, and Dexter Harbaugh are your clients, too."

"Yes, they are, and you'd do well to remember how successful they are as my clients." Nina flashed her ring at me again. "I've taken the matter in hand, Simon; never fear. I shall be among the speakers next week at Kinsale House. Lady Hermione has been after me for years, and I finally gave in. I shall be there to look after your interests, along with those of my other clients."

Struck by a sudden, horrid suspicion, I regarded Nina for a moment, like a rat waiting to be devoured by a python. "Tell me, dearest Nina, that you haven't hired this woman yourself." The latest Dorinda Darlington novel was set to be released in three weeks' time, and though sales of previous novels in the series had been terrific, growing with each new release, Nina had, from the first time I had met her, insisted they could be bigger and better. At our very first meeting, she had even suggested that I come out of the closet, so to speak, and admit publicly to being Dorinda. I refused point-blank, and she had, thankfully, dropped the idea.

Nina laughed. "No wonder, Simon, dearest, that you're such a successful mystery writer. You're so bloody devious, and you think the rest of the world is as devious as you are."

"Coming from you, Signorina Machiavelli, that's a compliment." I grinned at her. "But you didn't answer my question."

"Simon, what would I have to gain from such a tawdry stunt?" Nina pouted her lips at me. "The publicity campaign that Huddleston and Stourbridge have planned for the book is more than sufficient to put you high on the best-seller list, silly man. Not to mention the fact that it's a bloody good book."

"And you think that's going to be enough?"

"I've said so, haven't I, Simon?" Nina thumped the pile of papers on her desk. "About that manuscript I sent you, Simon. Did you read it, as I asked? Do you have a blurb to give me for it?"

"Yes, I read it, Nina, and I can't believe you asked me to waste my time on it." I pulled a sheet of paper from my jacket pocket. "What was the chap's name? Ashford Dunn. Who is this guy?"

"Didn't you read the letter and the accompanying material I sent with the manuscript, Simon?" Nina frowned at me.

I frowned right back at her. "There was a letter, a very brief one, but nothing else in the package except the manuscript."

Nina rolled her eyes. "Freddy! I should have known."

I hoped Freddy's other talents made up for his

deficiencies as an office assistant. "So what's the scoop on Dunn, Nina, and why should I have liked his book?"

"I do wish you had had the articles I wanted you to read, Simon. I don't have time for this!" Nina thumped her desk again. "Very well, Simon. Ashford Dunn is a young American lawyer, a very attractive young lawyer, who is about to be the biggest thing to hit the legal thriller market since Turow and Grisham."

"Nina, surely you read that manuscript you sent me? We can't be talking about the same person. It's bloody awful!"

"That has nothing to do with it, Simon. It's not the best legal thriller I've ever read, but this young man is going to be a huge star. He self-published his first novel when he was a student at some little midwestern American law school, and it sold quite well. An American publisher picked it up and published another one, and he almost made the *New York Times* list with it."

"And so you think he's poised on the brink of superstardom, just based on that?" I couldn't keep the skepticism from my voice.

Nina was practically purring with self-satisfaction as she shared her news with me. "Oh, he is, Simon. I've just signed a huge movie deal for him, plus an eight-figure advance for his next three books."

"Well, bully for him," I said, totally disgusted. "But I'm still not going to put my name on one of his books. Besides, if he's getting that kind of money from a publisher, what does he need my help for?"

Nina laughed. "I wasn't trying to help him, Simon. I was trying to help *you*. Especially since you've turned ed down my other proposals to make your name better known."

"I don't see where getting my name on a book I despised will do me any good."

"Fortunately, some of my other clients weren't quite so picky. In fact, Dexter Harbaugh was quite delighted to help out a rising young star."

"Somehow I'm not surprised that Dexter Harbaugh wouldn't mind putting his name on such tripe," I said. "Even though I must admit that Harbaugh's books are a cut or two above the swill that Dunn produced."

"Swill it might be, but it will sell. Absolutely pots and pots of lolly to be made, dear boy, and I shall enjoy raking it in. Ash wanted to break into the movies, and I've done it for him."

"And how did you discover such a treasure?"

"Through a mutual acquaintance who thought Ash has what it takes to make Grisham look like a has-been." She grinned. "I'd heard that one before, more times than I'd care to count, but once I caught a glimpse of Ash, I decided I wouldn't mind listening to his pitch."

It didn't take much imagination on my part to figure out which pitch had interested Nina the most. "So the young American lawyer hits the jackpot in London, eh, Nina?"

Nina affected not to notice the double entendre in my question. "Ash has the right formula, shall we say, and the ability to sell himself to an audience. The rest is just a matter of promotion."

I had had enough of Mr. Dunn. "So you say. But going back to a matter more pressing—to me, at least. What about this impostor?"

"I've already told you, Simon. You've nothing to worry about. I'll take care of everything." She flipped her hand at me in a dismissive gesture. "Now, go away and let me get to work."

Somewhat mollified, though not completely re-assured, I decided I would get nothing further from her. I'd be on my guard during the week at Kinsale House. Nina could be playing a very devious game, or she could have nothing to do with the impostor. Either way, it should prove to be an interesting week.

On Sunday afternoon, Giles and I loaded the car with luggage for our week's stay at Kinsale House and had a minor skirmish over who was going to drive. Giles insisted that he should, because it was what an assistant should do. I arched an eyebrow at that, and he treated me to one of his bad-boy grins. The poor boy drives a veritable antique, which is forever needing some kind of repair, and he can't resist any opportunity to get behind the wheel of my Jaguar.

"I don't doubt that I shall be the only writer at Kinsale House this week with a chauffeur-cum-executive-assistant who's a baronet," I said. "My, how intolerably high in the instep I've become."

Giles laughed. "You've been reading Georgette Heyer again, Simon."

Smiling, I handed him the keys and walked around to the passenger side of the car. Settling in and fastening my seat belt, I waited until Giles had adjusted everything to his satisfaction before I spoke again. "I know I needn't remind you, Giles, that you are not to lambaste the fake Dorinda Darlington the moment you meet her."

"I'll behave, Simon, as I promised you. I understand the need for discretion." He laughed. "Though I'd far rather threaten her with legal action for attempting to impersonate you. Or rather, one of your alter egos." He shook his head in disgust. "The sheer bloody effrontery of the woman!"

"I appreciate your loyalty, Giles, and I do admit that I'm excessively annoyed that someone would do such a thing." I stared out the window as the Jaguar moved smoothly down the lane through Snupperton Mumsley toward Kinsale House, several miles away. "But we need to get the lay of the land before I decide how to proceed. And Nina will be on hand as well."

Giles laughed. "With Freddy the boy toy in tow, one presumes?"

"Perhaps," I said.

"I wouldn't mind an hour or two alone with Freddy," Giles said in mock-salacious tones.

"I don't think he plays for our team," I said, smiling, "though I do admit he's rather luscious. As long, that is, as he keeps his mouth shut."

"He is rather stupid, isn't he?" Giles shook his head. "All his brains are in his—"

"Now, Giles," I interrupted, "no catty remarks like that around Nina, you hear me?"

He rolled his eyes at me, which meant that the Jag began drifting toward a hedgerow along the lane. Giles swore under his breath and righted the car.

"I debated whether we should actually stay at Kinsale House this week," I said. "I'm beginning to think, yet again, that we should have refused Lady Hermione's offer of rooms. I might feel more comfortable coming home each evening."

"Now, Simon," Giles said, mocking my earlier tone, "that just wouldn't do. One cannot turn down the offer of a week at Kinsale House."

I snorted rudely. "You mean you wouldn't be able to rub your mother's nose in it if we weren't staying there."

"Just an added benefit," Giles said airily.

"At least, if we're right on the spot for the whole week, I can keep an eye on pseudo-Dorinda more easily."

"Exactly," Giles said. "We have to watch your interests, Simon, and no better way to do it than to be right there, scrutinizing her every move."

"I appreciate your willingness to work so hard on my behalf, Giles," I said, teasing him.

His left hand strayed from the wheel and rested for a moment on my right knee. I let it stay there for a moment, then tapped it lightly with two fingers. "Keep your mind on your driving," I said, perhaps more sharply than I had intended.

Unrepentant, Giles gave my knee a quick squeeze before he put his hand back on the wheel, where it belonged. I sighed and stared out the window again. Giles frequently takes the opportunity to remind me that he finds me attractive and would welcome a more personal relationship. He is far too attractive for his own good, and he knows it; but thus far I've managed to resist his wiles, keeping our relationship firmly (or mostly firmly) on a business footing.

One of these days, however . . .

Fortunately for the sake of my wavering resolve, the lane to Kinsale House came into view, and Giles turned the car into it. As we drove onto the forecourt, we could see that another car had arrived before us. Dingleby, the butler, was assisting the driver from her car, a nondescript-looking Golf. Giles stopped the Jag a few feet behind the other car and shut off the engine. We alighted, and Giles stepped forward to offer his assistance to Dingleby.

The driver of the Golf, a plump, motherly-looking woman of fifty-odd—emphasis on the *odd*—appeared to have brought even more luggage than Giles and I between us. I stared in fascination as suitcase after suitcase was extracted from the car. How on earth had she managed to fit them all in there?

While Giles and Dingleby piled the suitcases beside the car, the driver walked around to the passenger side and opened the door. She leaned in and, as I craned my neck to see, appeared to be extracting a child from a car seat.

In haste, I moved forward to assist her, but I came up short as I realized what she was holding.

Cradled in her arms was a rather frowzy purple bunny. I watched, a bit stunned, as she stroked and petted the stuffed animal and spoke to it in low, soothing tones.

"There, there, Mr. Murbles, Mummy knows you don't like long drives, but we're here, aren't we, dearest? And soon we'll be in our room, and you can hop about to your heart's content and forget about being all cooped up in Mummy's horrid old car all the way from London. Won't that be lovely, dearest?"

Something sounding suspiciously like a snicker had emanated from Giles's direction, and I was hard pressed not to laugh myself. I had encountered a few eccentrics in my time, but this woman was angling for some sort of prize.

Not in the least abashed by my rather uncouth stare, the woman smiled at me and held out a hand. The other, needless to say, had cradled the cranky Mr. Murbles close to her ample bosom. "How do you do?" she said as I clasped her hand. "I'm Patty Anne Putney, and this is my dear friend, Mr. Murbles."

Since I had apparently overlooked the appropriate chapter in my Emily Post, I had no idea whether

I should try to shake the bunny's paw. One would so hate to be rude to a stuffed animal, after all. I settled for a bright smile and a nod. "Delighted to meet you both. I'm Simon Kirby-Jones, and this is my assistant, Giles Blitherington. Giles, do come and meet Miss Putney and Mr. Murbles."

While Giles was doing his best to keep a straight face, I glanced at Dingleby. I would have sworn he winked at me, but perhaps I imagined it. I suppose he had met Miss Putney and her dear friend before.

"And what do you write, Mr. Kirby-Jones?" Belatedly, I realized that Miss Putney had addressed me.

"I'm a historian, Miss Putney, and my specialty is medieval England. Lady Hermione was kind enough to invite me to Kinsale House this week to talk about historical fiction."

"How delightful!" She beamed at me, but Mr. Murbles was not in the least impressed. "I do believe I have read your biography of Eleanor of Aquitaine. Such an amazing woman, was she not?"

She couldn't be all that potty, I decided. "I do hope you enjoyed it, Miss Putney. Yes, she was extraordinary." I smiled modestly. "And of course, I am very familiar with your work. What mystery reader hasn't thrilled to the adventures of Miss Edwina Aiken and Hodge? Such a clever notion, an amateur sleuth assisted by her pet rooster."

Rather rudely dubbed by some as the "cock who . . ." series, the Hodge books had found an annual home on the best-seller lists on both sides of the Atlantic. No matter how twee some might find them, Miss Putney wrote with undeniable verve, and the books had their own peculiar charm. I had, after all, read three or four of them, so I must confess myself something of a fan.

After having met the author and her dear friend

Mr. Murbles, though, I had a new appreciation for the conversations in the books between Miss Aiken and Hodge. I guess they weren't tongue-in-cheek after all.

Miss Putney beamed at me. "How kind, Mr. Kirby-Jones. How very, very kind of you."

"Pardon me, ma'am," Dingleby spoke, "but if you don't mind, Lady Hermione awaits you in the drawing room."

"Of course, Dingleby," Miss Putney said. "Mr. Murbles can't wait to see his dearest auntie Hermione again, can you, my pet?"

Giles was suddenly overcome with a coughing fit as Miss Putney swept by him to follow Dingleby up the steps into Kinsale House. Trailing in her wake, I shook my head at Giles.

"I'll help Dingleby with the luggage, Simon," Giles called after me.

It would probably be just as well that Giles wouldn't be present to witness the no doubt touching reunion between Mr. Murbles and "Auntie" Hermione, though I was determined not to miss it myself.

I followed Miss Putney and her dearest through the front door of Kinsale House and through the hall to the drawing room. As we approached the door, it opened violently and almost hit Miss Putney and Mr. Murbles.

The man who barreled through the door came to an abrupt halt at the sight of Miss Putney. "Bloody cow!" He spat out the words.

Miss Putney slapped him.

Chapter Three

The sound of that slap reverberated through the hall, and I winced at the sharpness of it. I waited and watched to see what would happen next.

"Pig!" Miss Putney spat the word at the man she had just assaulted.

"If you *ever* do that again," the man said, his voice low and vicious, "I will take that absurd rabbit of yours and disembowel it."

"Oh, Dexter," Miss Putney moaned, clutching Mr. Murbles tightly against her bosom, "not even *you* could be that hideously cruel! You mustn't *ever* touch Mr. Murbles with anything but loving kindness."

While Miss Putney crooned and stroked her bunny, I examined her adversary with renewed interest. This, then, was the semilegendary Dexter Harbaugh. Dust jacket photos usually showed him in profile, his face shadowed, fedora pulled low, as befitted the author of a series of dark, cynical crime novels.

About six feet tall, lean, and fiftyish, he exuded meanness. Vampires are as sensitive to strong emotion as they are to sounds, and Dexter Harbaugh fairly dripped with nastiness. Not that this surprised me in the least, after having read three of his books. It seemed to me he hated everyone and everything, and his sleuth, Osgoode "Buster" Jones, lived up to his nickname in every book, thrashing and punching his way to a solution to each case. Few characters reached the end of a Harbaugh novel without a collection of bruises—those who weren't killed or maimed, that is.

Naturally, Harbaugh was a huge success, having won all the major awards in the mystery field. His gritty, no-holds-barred noir style tickled the critics and many of his peers, who touted Harbaugh's brand of realism as the ultimate expression of literary crime fiction. Feminists hated him because there were no intelligent women in his books; they were all bimbos, sluts, or whores, and they died in very unpleasant ways.

As Miss Putney stood quivering before him, Harbaugh reached out a hand and stroked her cheek. In addition to the nastiness he exuded, Harbaugh also gave off an aura of raw sexual energy. I felt Miss Putney respond, though reluctantly. There must be a story here, I thought.

"Oh, Dexter," Miss Putney moaned piteously. "Say you didn't mean it! Say you'd never hurt Mr. Murbles."

Harbaugh let out an exasperated breath. "Oh, you and your bloody rabbit!" He finally deigned to notice me. "Who the hell is this, Pattikins? Your latest?"

"Simon Kirby-Jones," I said coolly, extending a hand.

Harbaugh took it, then winced as I exerted pressure. His eyes widened, and he examined me with new interest. He flexed his fingers as he withdrew his hand from mine. "Hermione mentioned you just now," Harbaugh said. "You're a historian, she said."

I inclined my head. "My specialty is medieval England. Lady Hermione kindly invited me here to speak on the subject of historical fiction and research methods."

Harbaugh rolled his eyes. "Men poncing about in costumes, waving their swords, and women swooning at their feet. Surely you don't encourage that sort of mindlessness." He fixed Miss Putney with a pointed stare. "But the feminine mind, such as it is, seems to revel in all sorts of romantic nonsense."

What a prat, I thought. "Yes, the masculine mind is *much* tougher. It has to be concerned with convincing all and sundry of the size of its nether parts by beating up everyone in sight. Not to mention dehumanizing women and brutalizing anyone the least bit different."

I smiled sweetly as I said it, but I resisted the temptation to wink. Harbaugh reddened but forbore to respond. He pushed his way past me and Miss Putney and stalked away. I heard him clomping his way upstairs moments later as I offered Miss Putney my arm and escorted her into the drawing room to greet Lady Hermione.

Miss Putney had, to my great relief, stopped sniveling and greeted Lady Hermione and her timorous assistant, Mary Monkley, with a tremulous smile.

Lady Hermione wasted no time on the social amenities and instead barked out, "About time you got here! Monkley has your schedules, and if you've any questions, you will confer with her. Deviations from the schedule will cause problems, so tell her immediately if you discover any conflict."

Staring at the floor, Miss Monkley thrust a sheaf of papers in my general direction as my head began to ache. I had forgotten to stuff cotton in my ears to counteract the blast of Lady Hermione's voice, and I could feel a dull throb beginning between my eyes.

"Thank you, Lady Hermione, Miss Monkley," I said. "I shall examine these with all care and let you know if I see any potential problems. If, however, I might do so in my room, I'd very much appreciate it."

"Certainly," Lady Hermione boomed.

Miss Putney blew her nose on a handkerchief. "Hermione, dear, I really must get settled in my room. Mr. Murbles has had an upset, and he must have time to cleanse himself of the nasty negative energy to which he has been exposed."

"By all means," Lady Hermione said, and to my surprise, her pitch had softened to a normal level. "You and Mr. Murbles are in your favorite room. Would you mind terribly, my dear, showing Dr. Kirby-Jones his room? He is in the Gold Room, across the hall from you." She turned to me, and her decibel level rose with each syllable. "Your assistant, young Blitherington, will be in the dressing room attached to yours, Dr. Kirby-Jones. I trust he will find it sufficiently comfortable."

"No doubt he will," I said, though I wanted to suggest putting Giles farther away from me. There was no telling what he might try with the two of us in such proximity over the coming week. He really was incorrigible—and determined to get what he thought he wanted.

After sketching a courtly bow at Lady Hermione

and Miss Monkley, I followed Miss Putney from the room. The hallway was empty, and I figured Giles had gone on ahead to our rooms to begin unpacking. Glancing at my watch as I followed Miss Putney, I saw that it was time for one of the handy little pills that makes being a vampire a much less sanguinary task these days. Thanks to the marvels of modern science, three pills a day keep me from having, horror of horrors, to bite anyone on the neck and consume blood to maintain my existence. Those little pharmaceutical wonders, invented by government scientists back in the good old U.S. of A.—scientists who just happened to be vampires themselves, if you must know—have freed us from being creatures of the night and having to scurry from coffin to coffin, avoiding stake-wielding villagers and the like. I can no longer turn myself into a bat and fly, but who wants to be a bat, anyway?

Miss Putney, once we had reached the first floor, broke off her low-voiced conversation with Mr. Murbles long enough to point me toward the door of the Gold Room. I thanked her, and she smiled. With her help, Mr. Murbles waggled a paw in my direction. Evidently, he had already begun to cleanse himself of some of the negative energy; otherwise, I doubt he would have remembered his manners.

Or maybe I just bring out the best in stuffed animals.

My headache now gone, I opened the door to my room, then stood there, awestruck.

Imagine, if you will, what a room in an establishment of a certain kind, circa 1890, must have looked like. You know, the kind of establishment that catered to the appetites of repressed Victorian husbands seeking the type of attentions that their angels of

the hearth had been told no good woman even
knew about, much less desired to perform. There
was gold everywhere: gold carpet, gold draperies,
gold coverlets, pillows, and upholstery, occasionally
relieved by red with dashes of green. Nearly everything had a fringe of some sort, and if it had no
fringe, it had tassels. The wallpaper was gold with a
pattern of blood-red flowers, and the furniture was
gilt.

"Now I'm beginning to understand," Giles said
from across the room, "why Kinsale House is very
rarely featured in any of the leading design maga-
zines."

I shut the door behind me. "It's perfectly hideous,
isn't it?"

"Too bordello for words." Giles laughed. "Wait
till I tell Mummy about this!"

"I wouldn't," I said. "Next thing you know, she'll
want to redo your ancestral manor to look just like
it."

"Point well taken." He laughed again. He beck-
oned me toward the doorway in which he stood.
"Thankfully, my own little nook is Spartan by com-
parison."

Crossing the room, dodging around the canopied
bed, I came to stand beside him. The dressing room,
only about a quarter the size of the bedchamber,
was sparsely and plainly furnished. "Small, but much
easier on the eyes—and the stomach," I said.

"You're welcome to join me, Simon," he said,
one arm snaking around my waist. "The bed's a bit
small, but no doubt it could accommodate two, if
you find yourself overwhelmed by the horrors of
your room."

"I won't be able to see it with the lights off," I said
lightly, moving away from him. I could hear the in-

take of an exasperated breath, but he ought to be used to it by now. "Patience, Giles, patience."

"So you keep saying, Simon," he said, offering me a cheeky grin.

"Finish your unpacking while I take care of mine," I said, smiling briefly in return. "Then we'll go down and meet the rest of the guests."

In about twenty minutes I had my clothes and various other articles neatly stowed away. Someone at Kinsale House had thoughtfully provided several bottles of water and a tray of clean glassware, so I didn't have to head down the hall to the loo to get drinking water. I couldn't forget my little pill any longer.

While I waited for Giles to finish—he's a bit of a tidiness freak and must have things just so—I sorted through the stack of partial manuscripts I'd been asked to evaluate. I had meant to tackle them before arriving at Kinsale House, but I hadn't found the energy to do so. I'd have to read and critique them tonight, while everyone else was in the land of Nod. I could probably get through the nine I had been given by morning.

"I must say, Simon," Giles said, coming to stand near the bed where I had perched, "you are gazing upon those manuscripts with all the enthusiasm of the Labour Party welcoming Margaret Thatcher at a fund-raiser."

I shrugged. "I've done this once or twice before, Giles, and I have a good idea what to expect. One of them, if I'm lucky, will be quite good. Most will be mediocre at best, and one or two will probably be perfectly dreadful. The trick is to offer sound criticism without destroying a writer's fragile ego."

"If they're that dreadful," Giles said, "think of it as euthanasia."

"I'm sure the writers would be most comforted to hear you say that," I said wryly, standing up. "Enough of that. Let's wend our way back downstairs. After having met Miss Putney, Mr. Murbles, and Dexter Harbaugh, I'm desperately curious to see what other delightful personalities are on hand for the week."

Giles was curious about Dexter Harbaugh, and as we proceeded out into the hall I gave him a quick précis of my encounter with the nasty Mr. H. As we approached the stairs, one of the doors near them opened, and a stately elderly woman, followed by a younger portly man several inches shorter than she, stepped in front of us. She was so involved in her conversation with her companion that she failed to take note of Giles and me.

"What you say could be true, George, but that doesn't alter my feelings in the least. I shall say it again. I'll see the bitch in hell first!"

Chapter Four

Afterward, I could have dined out on the story that Isabella Veryan, grande dame of the British crime novel, had uttered a vulgarity. After all, one doesn't expect such language from the woman who is one of the world's most revered mystery writers. Though on occasion one of her characters has used such a word, these instances are all the more shocking for their infrequency—something Dexter Harbaugh might consider.

With remarkable composure Miss Veryan faced Giles and me. "I do beg your pardon," she said, her voice frosty.

"But of course, Miss Veryan," I said in my smoothest tones, before she could launch into an explanation or a further apology. "What a pleasure it is to meet you! I'm a great admirer of your work, and I have been looking forward to telling you, in person, how many hours of pleasure your books have given me."

"Thank you," she said, the frost melting noticeably. "One never tires of hearing such words. But I fear you have the advantage of me."

"I beg your pardon," I said. "I should have introduced myself properly. Simon Kirby-Jones, historian, at your service, Miss Veryan. And may I present my assistant, Giles Blitherington?"

Giles clasped the proffered hand and smiled with every ounce of his considerable charm as he murmured a greeting. She thawed even further.

Beside her, her diminutive companion was growing restive. Miss Veryan collected herself and released Giles's hand. I'd have to tease him later about his latest conquest.

"George Austen-Hare," said Miss Veryan's companion, his voice booming out. "How d'ye do?" He shook hands in turn with Giles and me.

"Again, it's a great pleasure, sir," I said, gazing down into his eyes. "I have spent many an hour visiting one exotic locale after another in your company. Your books have an incredible sense of place."

Giles and I were batting a thousand in the charm department this afternoon. Austen-Hare beamed as widely as Miss Veryan had done, and I noted with amusement that he couldn't resist casting her a triumphant glance.

They made an odd couple: she, tall and thin; he, short and chubby. He could have gotten steady work as a garden gnome if he ever got desperate, but a string of best-selling novels had made that unlikely. Under the name of Victoria Whitney-Stewart he wrote tales of romance and intrigue set all over the world. In his books intrepid young women, seeking their place in the world, encountered danger at every turn but somehow managed to survive, and in the end walked off into the sunset of Happily Ever After with a handsome man. Austen-Hare had only recently admitted to the pseudonym, and the news that a former London postman had penned these books had been a nine-days' wonder in the literary world. His sales had shot up even further. Nina Yaknova, his agent and mine, had no doubt been delighted that her publicity campaign had paid off so handsomely.

"Delighted," said Austen-Hare, his voice gruff with pleasure. He all but preened in front of us. "Great fun, writing those books, don't ye know."

"And they're even more fun to read," I assured him, and I swear his chest puffed up even further.

"Kirby-Jones," Miss Veryan said in a reflective tone, examining me as one might a specimen under a microscope. "Ah, yes, that marvelous biography of Eleanor of Aquitaine. You write history, Dr. Kirby-Jones, as entertainingly as one writes fiction. Quite a knack you have."

Now it was my turn to preen a bit. I'm not in the least immune to flattery, especially coming from so august a source. "Thank you, Miss Veryan. I'm delighted to know that you've read my work."

"Tedious woman," Austen-Hare sniffed, and I wasn't sure whether he was referring to Miss Veryan or that long-dead queen. Either way, it was rude.

"I beg your pardon," I said, my tone stiff with umbrage.

"Coming our way," Austen-Hare muttered. "Down the hall."

We turned as one, and approaching us from the other end of the hall, jerking along like a stork with sore feet, came a vision in iridescent silk. Her particolored dress dazzled our eyes, and a wave of cloying, overly sweet perfume reached us several feet ahead of the woman herself. She wormed her way in between Miss Veryan and Austen-Hare and stopped, beaming at each of us in turn. Not so tall as Miss Veryan, she yet loomed over Austen-Hare, on whom her gaze came to rest adoringly. "How lovely to find you all here—especially you, Mr. Austen-Hare. You are such an inspiration to us all, you know."

Her voice, textbook nasal, had ambitions of Oxbridge, carefully layered over a bedrock of broad Yorkshire. The combination was disconcerting, and Miss Veryan winced.

"Norah, what a pleasure," Austen-Hare said with a noticeable lack of enthusiasm. "Should have figured you'd be here. You always are."

Giles and I waited for someone to do the polite thing, but Miss Veryan seemed overcome and had stepped away, while Austen-Hare continued to gaze balefully at the newcomer.

Suppressing a sigh, I stuck out my hand. "How do you do? I'm Simon Kirby-Jones, and this is Giles Blitherington."

She wrenched her attention away from Austen-Hare and focused on me. "Norah Tattersall," she said, grasping my hand in a firm grip. "*Miss* Norah Tattersall. Very pleased to make your acquaintance, I'm sure." She batted her eyelashes at Giles. "And what do you write?"

I explained my presence at the conference, and Giles confessed, modestly for him, to being my assistant.

"I'm sure your lecture will be terribly interesting, Mr. Kirby-Jones," Norah Tattersall said, beaming at me. "Dear Lady Hermione never asks anyone who isn't absolutely top drawer. Perhaps you shall inspire me to try my hand at historical fiction. Deciding on a period is such a trial, though. There are so many fascinating times in history that one could explore, and I'm rather afraid I should have a hard time settling on just the right one."

Miss Veryan suppressed a sound suspiciously like a snort, while Austen-Hare coughed. "That can indeed be a trial, Miss Tattersall," I said.

"How *is* your novel these days, Norah?" Miss Veryan asked, her tone sugary sweet. "Have you finished the first draft yet?" Without giving Miss Tattersall time to answer, Miss Veryan turned to me. "Dear Norah is *such* a perfectionist, Dr. Kirby-Jones. She's. been working on her crime novel for the past ten years or so, haven't you, Norah, dear? And she's so determined to get everything *just* right. I quite admire your fortitude."

The sarcasm in Miss Veryan's tone would have shriveled me, but Norah Tattersall appeared proof against it. "One learns so many things at these conferences, doesn't one? I find myself looking back over what I've done, in the light of the wisdom of writers more experienced than I, and I can't help but want to go back and fix things. I shall finish it, one of these days."

"I'm sure we all look forward to that day, Norah," Miss Veryan said. "If, indeed, such a day *ever* comes."

"If I should decide to write a historical novel," Miss Tattersall said, facing Miss Veryan with a sweet smile, "perhaps I'll write about England before the First World War. I'm sure, Dame Isabella, that you'd be happy to tell me what it was like back then, wouldn't you?" Turning away from the outraged look on Miss Veryan's face, Miss Tattersall addressed me. "After all, Mr. Kirby-Jones, isn't it best, when researching such a period, to talk to those who have lived through it?"

I had to admire the cool effrontery of Miss Tattersall's insult. Miss Veryan had been born nearly a decade after the end of that particular war, which fact Miss Tattersall no doubt knew very well. But how could I respond, with any tact, to such a question?

Miss Tattersall saved me the necessity of such an impossible task. "I do believe Lady Hermione is expecting us downstairs," she said, tucking her hand into the crook of Austen-Hare's arm and commencing to drag him toward the stairs. "We must go and greet the others."

I offered my arm to Miss Veryan and pretended not to see the look of hatred she aimed at Miss Tattersall's retreating back. I figured I'd best hold on to her, to keep her from pushing the younger woman down the stairs in view of us all. Being a witness at the ensuing trial would be so tedious.

"How unutterably common," Miss Veryan commented, *sotto voce,* as she placed her hand lightly upon my arm. "But then, what more can one expect of the daughter of a man who made a fortune manufacturing toilet brushes?"

I recalled having read somewhere that Miss Veryan's father had been the younger son of a duke.

As we descended the stairs, Giles trailing dutifully behind us, I kept Miss Veryan distracted by babbling on and on about one of her most famous novels, *A Doubtful Joy,* one of my all-time favorite crime novels. By the time we joined the others in the drawing room, Miss Veryan was practically purring, having told me twice how much she appreciated my astute analysis of her work. A little charm works wonders, all the more so when it's based on sincere feelings.

Lady Hermione was holding court amidst a small crowd of milling conference-goers. George Austen-Hare had, none too gracefully, wiggled loose from Norah Tattersall's tight grasp and gone off to accost several young women who had gathered together on one side of the room. Miss Tattersall, thus abandoned, cast about for a moment but quickly latched on to someone she evidently recognized.

Lady Hermione hailed us from across the room, and her voice, as usual, boomed out over the noise generated by the twenty or so people in the room with her. "Isabella, my dear! I see you've met Dr. Kirby-Jones and his assistant." She motioned with her left hand while her right kept a tight grasp on the arm of her companion, a handsome man in his late twenties. "Do let me introduce you to another guest who's here for his first visit with us."

Our little threesome halted before Lady Hermione and her companion, whose identity I had already guessed. Ashford Dunn, Nina's newest client, the new blazing star of the legal thriller genre, stood appraising us with a cool gaze. I could see at a glance why Nina had signed him. He had the chiseled good looks of the proverbial matinee idol, and from his stance, he also possessed the cockiness to go with them. He couldn't write worth a damn, but when had that ever stopped someone from becoming a best-seller? Image these days seemed much more important than content, and Dunn had an image that could sell, and sell big. Nina was no fool.

Lady Hermione introduced us with the air of a general reviewing her troops, and I gave Dunn's hand a quick shake. He couldn't resist trying to turn it into a power contest, the silly man, and I exerted just enough pressure to make him wince. To him I might look a bit on the effete side, but then, he had no idea what I really was. To him I looked human. To me he looked intelligent.

After a startled, slightly resentful glance at me, he passed on to Giles. As he shook Giles's hand and acknowledged his rather cool greeting, Dunn let his eyes wander back and forth between Giles and me, and I could see in his eyes that he had decided that we had something more than an employer-employee relationship. His lip curled slightly as he turned away to fawn over Miss Veryan, dismissing Giles and me as of no importance whatsoever.

"I've read all your books several times, Miss Veryan," Dunn said, his voice silky, the midwestern flat tones very pronounced. "I can say without exaggerating that you've been a big influence on my own writing. For example, in my first book, *Presumed Guilty,* I set my murder during a production of *Hamlet,* like the brilliant way you did the same thing in *The Skull Beneath the Skin.* "

Giles laughed aloud before he could stop himself, and I almost did the same thing. The look on Miss Veryan's face would have frozen boiling water, but Dunn nattered on, totally oblivious. He was too caught up in regaling us with the ingenious way he had used the plot of a Shakespearean play in his novel to pay attention to Giles's open mirth at his expense.

Miss Veryan, after a few moments of outraged silence, cut in on his smug blather. "If you're going to try to suck up to someone, young man, you might at least make the effort to do so in an intelligent manner." With that, she turned and swept off, leaving an openmouthed Dunn in her wake. Lady Hermione cast a glare at her young guest as she went after Miss Veryan, leaving a bewildered Dunn to my tender mercies.

"What the hell did I say to make the old biddy so angry?" Dunn asked, his face twisted in a grimace of distaste.

"Miss Veryan didn't write *The Skull Beneath the Skin,*" I informed him, trying not to smirk as his eyes grew wide with horror. "P. D. James did. And wasn't the play Webster's *The Duchess of Malfi?*"

"Damn!" Dunn said, adding several rather colorful vulgarities under his breath. "I can't tell those old women apart. All their books are the same. Page after page after page of some detective brooding about life and wondering why the vicar forgot to put the dog out. I could never make it all the way through a single one of those books."

"No one to help you with the big words?" Giles said, his tone oozing mock sympathy.

In a nasty tone, Dunn suggested that Giles do something physically impossible to accomplish—unless one is a freak of nature, that is—then stalked off.

"How utterly charming," Giles said, not in the least bothered by Dunn's behavior.

"You missed your chance to make a handsome new friend," I said, smiling. "And here I thought he'd be just your type."

He rolled his eyes at me. "You're not going to foist me off on a prat like that, Simon. Never fear."

"One can always hope," I said. He rewarded me with a raised eyebrow.

Before the discussion could degenerate any further, Lady Hermione once again hailed me.

I turned to see her approaching with an attractive young woman in tow. "Let me introduce you," Lady Hermione boomed, "to the final member of our staff for this week. Dr. Kirby-Jones, this is Dorinda Darlington, the mystery writer. Dorinda, my dear, Simon Kirby-Jones, our historical expert, and his assistant, Giles Blitherington."

My senses went on high alert at hearing that name. Here was the impostor, in the too, too-solid flesh. Would she exude any guilt or nervousness at meeting me, whose identity she had appropriated?

Chapter Five

Cool as a cucumber, this faux Dorinda was. She gave off no feelings of nervousness or trepidation at meeting me. Upon reflection, I realized that she might have no idea who the real "Dorinda" was. My identity had been a closely guarded secret, known heretofore only to my agents and my editors back in the United States and here in England. Unless one of them were complicit in this masquerade, faux Dorinda couldn't have figured it out.

"How do you do, Miss Darlington?" I said, as smoothly as I could manage over the raging irritation I felt at meeting her. "I have enjoyed your books very much. I thought your first novel, *Alibi for Murder,* was exceptionally polished for a debut novel."

"Thank you," she said, smiling. "But actually, that was my second book. *Crime on Her Mind* was my first novel."

A point to her for neatly sidestepping that trap—she had at least done her homework. "Ah, yes, I stand corrected, Miss Darlington. Tell me, though, isn't there a new novel due soon? Your fans, myself included, are impatient for a new one."

She smiled again. "I'm delighted to say that my fourth book, *An Overture to Murder,* will be out in a couple of weeks."

"What an intriguing title," I said. "Tell me, if you will, what the background for this story is. With a title like that, is it something to do with music?"

"Yes, opera, actually," she replied. "One of my interests."

More points for that one. Of course, such information wouldn't be that difficult to come by. There had been a glowing review in *Publishers Weekly* and one or two in the British press already, which gave enough of the plot details. Whatever her game was, she was certainly well prepared.

I observed her for a few moments while she chatted with Lady Hermione and Giles. If I had had to choose someone to portray "Dorinda" publicly, I would not have picked someone like her. Upon closer inspection, she was not as attractive as I had first thought, though she did have alert, intelligent eyes. Short blond hair framed her head in oddly angled spikes, while an overly generous mouth made her face seem out of proportion. *Plain* was the most charitable adjective I could use to describe her.

The faux Dorinda focused intently on what Giles was saying—something about the new book—and her eyes sparkled as she looked at him. For that I couldn't blame her; he is quite delicious, and when he sets out to charm someone, he usually manages to do so.

It wouldn't do to underestimate her as an adversary. What her particular game was, I had no idea, but before this week was over, I would find out.

"What will you be speaking on this week, Miss Darlington?" I asked during a lull in her conversation with Giles.

"Call me Dorinda, please," she said. "Lady Hermione has asked me to talk about contemporary women sleuths, and how to create a strong, intelligent, and multidimensional character."

"Based on what I've read of your work," Giles said, "you certainly know whereof you speak. Your heroine is a marvelously realized character."

I almost said, "Thank you," but fortunately, faux Dorinda beat me to it before I could give the game away. As she accepted Giles's compliment, I surreptitiously squeezed his hand, and he squeezed back to acknowledge it.

"Is Dorinda Darlington your real name?" I asked. "I was just curious, if you don't mind my asking. Sometimes writers choose to cloak their identities in pseudonyms, and the biographical information on your book jackets is rather sketchy, after all."

She was not in the least disconcerted by my question. "It is a pseudonym," she replied, "because I do like my privacy. I've only recently decided to begin making public appearances, and while I'm in the public eye, I prefer to be known as Dorinda. I'm sure you will understand."

"But of course," I said. I'd find out, somehow, what her real name was, and before much longer. She certainly wasn't going to tell me. "Another thing that occurs to me, now that I've met you: isn't it rather unusual for an English-woman to write a series about an American female private eye? How did you come to do that?"

"I lived in America for several years," she responded, her tone cool, "and I've always been fascinated by American crime fiction." She preened a bit. "And thus far, no one has been able to detect that I'm not American."

"Amazing, isn't it?" I said, though something in my tone must have gotten through to her. Her eyes narrowed a moment as she examined my face.

"Now, if you'll excuse me," faux Dorinda said, making a move away from our small group, "I really must go and talk with Dame Isabella Veryan. We have the same agent, and I've been dying to meet her."

Interesting. She knows about Nina, I thought. *I wonder what that could mean. . . .*

Lady Hermione had already wandered off, and Giles and I were left alone together in the midst of the group. "What do you think, Simon? What is she after?" he asked in a low voice.

I shrugged. "I'm not sure yet. We'll both have to be on the alert this week and try to ferret out anything we can about her. She obviously has done her best to learn as much as she can, especially if she knows that Nina is the agent representing the Dorinda books. I want to know why she's doing this, and what she expects to gain from it. Then I can decide how I want to handle the situation."

Giles began to speak, but I held up a hand to forestall him. Dorinda and Dame Isabella had moved closer to us, and I wanted to hear what they were saying. It took a bit of focusing to filter out the extraneous noise from all the conversations buzzing around us, but I managed to concentrate enough to hear most of what they were saying. Giles waited patiently. He had seen me eavesdropping before.

". . . do wish you would reconsider my request, Dame Isabella," Dorinda was saying.

"I have already told you at least twice, young woman," Miss Veryan said, at her frostiest, "that I will not do such a thing. I've also informed Nina that I find your importuning disgraceful. I still can't believe you had the nerve to show up, uninvited, on my doorstep as you did last week. There's no use your continuing to badger me in this way. Had I known you were to be here this week, I would have sent my regrets to Hermione."

"But you *are* here," Dorinda replied smoothly, "and I'm sure that before the week is over, you will see things my way. After all, I'm sure it wouldn't do to have the reading public to know every little thing about the past of the revered crime novelist Dame Isabella Veryan."

The mockery in her tone as she said "every little thing" and "revered" was enough to set my teeth on edge, and I could imagine how it affected Miss Veryan. I had turned my head slightly, and I could see that she had turned white with suppressed fury.

"You vulgar, self-seeking little bitch," Miss Veryan said, biting off the words. "How dare you threaten me! Do you think I would fall for such empty threats?"

Dorinda laughed—not a pleasant sound. "I'm sure you will agree, Dame Isabella, that parish records can be so very, very interesting. Particularly the records I happened to run across in a rather out-of-the-way little church in East Anglia."

"Go to hell!" Miss Veryan said.

"Now, do you really think that's polite?" Dorinda said, her calm unruffled. "I never knew you had such a temper, dear Dame Isabella. But then, there's so much about you that many others *don't* know, isn't there?"

By then, however, she was talking to the air, for

Miss Veryan had whirled on one heel and stalked away from her. I turned to stare at Dorinda, fascinated. It's not often that one hears such blatant attempts at blackmail, and in so public a gathering.

Dorinda must have felt the force of my gaze on her, because she turned and looked me straight in the eyes. She smiled mockingly, then turned away. The gauntlet had been thrown down, so to speak.

"Simon!" I felt Giles's hand on my arm. "What was it? What did you hear?" He has noticed, of course, that I have very keen hearing, but he has no idea why.

I turned back to him and quickly repeated the gist of the conversation. He grimaced when I had finished. "So that's part of her game, eh? Blackmail!" He frowned. "Wonder what it is that she wants Miss Veryan to do."

"Whatever it is, Miss Veryan doesn't seem inclined to play along," I said. "But that will depend on just how embarrassed Miss Veryan is over this supposed secret Dorinda claims to have uncovered."

"There must be something to it," Giles said, "or Miss Veryan would have reacted differently, don't you think? She didn't really deny anything."

"No, she didn't," I said, considering. "We'll have to keep that in mind."

Further speculation became impossible because a couple of the conference attendees approached us at that point. Evidently, George Austen-Hare had explained to several of the young women with whom he had been flirting just who I was, and two of them had come over to express their admiration for my work. While Giles glowered quietly at them and their attempts to flirt with me, I enjoyed the attention and Giles's manifestation of jealousy. The dear boy has become much too proprietary toward me, and I refuse to indulge him. He'll have to get over such behavior if he's going to be around for very long.

For the next half hour or so, I worked the room, moving from one group to the next, Giles dogging my heels, getting to know the various conference attendees. Though the group was largely female, several of the men were quite attractive, and Giles became even more taciturn as I chatted with some of them. Poor boy! He's so terribly obvious, and for all his sophistication in other matters, in this he's still quite callow.

I was quite enjoying my conversation with a distinguished-looking older man, probably in his late fifties, when I saw Norah Tattersall finally managing to corner George Austen-Hare nearby. She had been trying for some time, quite unsuccessfully, to get him alone, but the last of the attractive young women in the room had finally eluded him, and Norah had seized her chance. While I listened with what appeared to be full attention to my conversational partner of the moment, I focused in on the chat taking place a few feet away from us, in an alcove by one of the windows in the room.

"You're not returning my calls, Georgie," Norah said, her voice becoming even more unpleasant as it took on a distinct whine.

"Told you, Norah," Austen-Hare replied gruffly, "that it's all over between us. Mistake in the first place—very obvious to me. Should have been to you, as well."

"Now, Georgie, don't say such cruel things," Norah cried. "You know how much I adore you!"

"Georgie" harrumphed. "Absolute balderdash, Norah, and you know it! All you want is to get that blasted book of yours published. Don't know why you don't just publish it yourself! Certainly have the money, don't you!" With that, he squirmed out of her grasp and stalked away from her, leaving her openmouthed and sniffling.

Unnoticed by me, Dorinda had been skulking nearby, and she chose this moment to intercept George, who looked anything but pleased to see her. Norah wandered away, dabbing at her nose with a handkerchief. I had been trying to keep an eye on Dorinda as she worked the room. A few minutes earlier I had spotted her in conversation with Ashford Dunn. I hadn't been close enough to hear what they were saying, but if I was any judge of body language, Dunn didn't seem any more enamored of Dorinda than her other targets had been. Was she trying her hand at blackmailing all the authors present?

My companion had by then realized my distraction, and fearing that he would find me rude, I forced my complete attention back to him. With an apologetic smile, I encouraged him to continue a description of his work-in-progress. Giles, who had wandered away to find something to drink, came back just then, and I had no further chance to eavesdrop.

Though I was no longer hearing what was going on with George, I could at least see that George didn't seem any fonder of Dorinda than Miss Veryan had been. Somehow I'd have to find out what it was that Dorinda had said to make George's face take on such an alarming shade of red.

Chapter Six

Later that same evening, when I had finally gained the dubious refuge of my hideous bedroom, I settled down to read through the manuscripts I had been assigned to critique. They were not an especially prepossessing lot, as I had discovered. There were nine in all, and out of the batch one was very promising, and two or three had problems that were fixable, if their authors were willing to listen to constructive criticism. But the rest—well, the rest were ample evidence of what Alexander Pope wrote: "Hope springs eternal . . ."

The hours slipped by as I worked. The good ones had been easy enough to critique, as is usually the case. The others were much more problematic, at least from my point of view. How could I address the manifest problems in any constructive way without discouraging the authors? Some—and here I was thinking of curmudgeonly Dexter Harbaugh—

would no doubt revel in the chance to say nasty things, but I couldn't bring myself to do it, no matter how tempted I might be. It would definitely be easier to ridicule than to try to instruct, but the instinct to teach was too ingrained in me, though it had been a while since I had been active in the role of teacher. Thanks to various circumstances—not the least of which was the whole vampire thing—I had been able to give up teaching rather early in my career and focus instead on writing.

I sat and glared at one of the manuscripts on the desk and front of me. It had been every bit as dire as I had been warned it would be. Earlier in the evening, Isabella Veryan had caught me alone for a moment amid the group.

"Simon," she said, for by that time we had progressed to first names—the more sherry she imbibed the more casual she became, it seemed—"a word of warning, dear boy." With her head cocked to one side and her gaze turning glassy from the sherry, she resembled nothing so much as a slightly tipsy parrot.

"Yes, Isabella, what is it?" I prompted when she fell silent.

"What?" She forced herself to focus. "Oh, yes, a warning—definitely a warning is in order." Her diction was as precise as ever. "Since you're the new chappie here, no doubt Hermione has saddled you with the albatross." She giggled, then covered her mouth with her free hand. "Oh, dear, I really shouldn't say such things."

"What albatross would that be, Isabella?" I asked, hiding a smile.

"Bloody Norah's bloody book," she hissed, peering around as if fearing to be overheard. "It is singularly without merit, the most sick-making combination of utter tripe and bloody nonsense you'll ever hope to read."

"Well, thank you for the warning," I said slowly, watching her, fearing that she might tip over, from the way she had begun to sway back and forth.

"Not at all, dear boy, not at all. You are most welcome." She leaned in closer to me, and I drew in a breath rich with the fumes of Jerez. "Just wanted to let you know, don't worry about sparing Norah's feelings when you critique the bloody thing." She paused to cover her mouth as she belched discreetly. "Woman hasn't got a sensitive bone in her whole body, so it won't matter if you savage her. With all her millions, what does she care?"

After that, Miss Veryan had tottered away, leaving me puzzled in my corner of the room. What, besides apparently sheer malice, had been the point of that little conversation? Could Norah Tattersall's book really be *that* bad?

Now, bleary-eyed at four in the morning, I knew Isabella hadn't been exaggerating. Norah Tattersall's manuscript was, without doubt, the single worst piece of utter nothingness I had ever read in my life. If anything, Isabella had been kind in her assessment. If Norah had *ever* had an original thought in her life, it had died long ago for lack of companionship. Everything in her book was derivative, and, even worse, derivative of books that weren't that good at the outset.

The subjects and verbs of most of the sentences (at least, those sentences which actually *had* subjects and verbs) agreed—I'd have to give her that much. But beyond that, the writing was just plain godawful. Next to Norah, a writer like James Corbett seemed Nobel Prize material.

To think that the woman had been working on

this same book, year after year after year—well, it really didn't bear contemplation. Could someone be *that* blind? *That* stupid? *That* masochistic? When I had seen her earlier, in interaction with George Austen-Hare and Isabella Veryan, she had certainly seemed sharper than this manuscript evinced. But, as I well knew, when it came to writing, a person could be very different on paper from how she appeared in the flesh.

I shook my head in a vain attempt to rid it of some of Norah's dreadful prose. She had described one character as "a man with a face that could stop a clock, but not just any clock, he could probably have stopped Big Ben he was so ugly, but women nevertheless found something attractive about him, like he was one of those men you see on the telly selling something to bored housewives in Clapham who have nothing better to do."

And that was one of the *good* sentences.

Faced with evaluating something this dreadful, I regretted ever having agreed to take part in this conference in the first place. Not that, as I recalled, I had had much choice about participating. Hurricane Hermione had swept me along in her path, and now I had to sort through the mess. I sighed and picked up a pen. What on earth could I say to this woman about her wretched manuscript? Was there any bit of criticism to which she would pay the slightest bit of attention?

I doubted it. If she had persisted this long, rewriting this drivel over and over again for years, she was obviously proof against any kind of criticism, constructive or destructive, for that matter.

After pondering it for a few minutes longer, I finally gave up without writing anything on her evaluation form. Perhaps I'd come up with something by the time I had to meet with her to discuss the manuscript. I shuddered at the thought. How could I ever look the woman in the face again after having read this mess of pottage?

"Still awake, Simon?"

Giles's voice, heavy with sleep, jerked me out of my reverie. I looked up from the desk, turning my head toward the sound of his voice. He was leaning against the door leading from my bedroom into his.

"Giles," I said, my voice deceptively mild, "why are you standing there naked?"

In the dim light of the reading lamp, the only illumination in the room, I could see his smile—and pretty much everything else, including the dragon tattoo that covers a goodly portion of his back, one arm and shoulder, and his chest. Need I say that his mother has no idea he has a tattoo, or else she'd be pushing up daisies in the churchyard at St. Athelwold's in Snupperton Mumsley?

"I always sleep this way, Simon," Giles said, reaching down to scratch himself in what I'm sure he thought was a provocative manner. The dragon stretched in a sinuous movement.

"Giles," I said, this time with a peremptory note in my voice, "what have I told you about such behavior?"

He didn't pretend to misunderstand, because he knew it wouldn't wash with me. "Really, Simon, you are the absolute limit sometimes!" He turned and pulled the door shut behind him.

Laughing quietly, I turned off the light and sought my own bed.

Some three hours later, I awoke, feeling much refreshed. Thankfully, vampires require little sleep, and I can even go several days without any, but I tend to start looking a bit haggard without it. I dislike looking haggard.

A clock in the hallway had just chimed seven-thirty when I finished dressing. I downed my morning pill, then strode across the room to open Giles's door and peek inside. He was sound asleep, which was just as well. He is excellent company most of the time, and he's most efficient at his job, but one can occasionally have too much of a good thing.

Downstairs there were quite a number of people already milling about, heading for the dining hall. I say *hall* rather than *room*, because it was a very large chamber, capable of seating about a hundred people. Now there were only about a dozen, among whom Lady Hermione, thankfully, did not number. It was too early for an assault on my eardrums.

I helped myself to small portions of eggs, bacon, and toast from the sideboard and found a seat. Vampires don't require much in the way of food as sustenance, but breakfast has always been my favorite meal. I still enjoy the sensuousness of eating, and the cook at Kinsale House had provided fluffy scrambled eggs and bacon cooked just the way I like it. Add to that toast laden with butter and homemade black-currant jam, and I was as near to heaven as a vampire can get. I also have to admit to enjoying the fact that I won't gain any weight, no matter what I consume. Hateful, isn't it?

As I slowly savored and consumed my rather meager helpings, I chatted with the woman sitting to my left. She confided shyly that she was an aspiring writer of historical romance novels, and when I responded with interest rather than disdain, she blossomed, telling me about her work. Hers, as it turned out, was the best manuscript in the group I had been asked to evaluate, and I told her how much promise I thought it had. We spent a happy half hour talking about romance fiction in general, and hers in particular, and she quite won me over when she mentioned that yours truly, in my guise of Daphne Deepwood, was one of her favorite writers.

This pleasant interlude came to an abrupt halt with the appearance of Lady Hermione in the dining hall. Her voice preceded her, naturally. I think the woman could easily be heard over a heavy metal rock group at its loudest. I shuddered and shrank back against my chair.

Rather quickly—but politely, I hoped—I excused myself from my breakfast companion and made my escape before Lady Hermione could approach me. She had a certain gleam in her eye when she espied me at the table, but fortunately for me, one of the conference attendees claimed her attention, and I got out of there like the proverbial bat out of hell.

And ran right smack-dab into Dorinda, knocking her flat on her plagiarizing posterior.

Chapter Seven

If one were going to be literally correct, Dorinda wasn't a plagiarist. She *was* an impostor, however, who lay stunned on the floor while I loomed over her.

Let me amend that to *stunned and furious*.

She recovered quickly. "Why don't you watch the hell where you're going, you big oaf!" She was sitting up and describing me and my ancestry with a string of invective as fluent as it was repetitive.

"I do beg your pardon," I said, my tone as cool as I could manage as I extended a hand to help her up. She pulled hard at me, as if trying to jerk me down onto the floor, but I easily countered that and had her up on her feet before she realized what was happening. She did not appear in the least grateful.

"Apology accepted," she said grudgingly.

"Thank you," I responded. Having to apologize

to her for any reason irked me considerably, because I felt I was being done the far more grievous wrong. Her very presence here offended me. But I couldn't address that just yet.

"I thought I might attend your session this morning," I said in as placatory a tone as I could manage, "because I'm very curious to hear what you have to say about writing mysteries with a hard-boiled female sleuth."

"I'm sure you'll learn something," she said coolly as she dusted off her slacks. "This is my first writers' conference, but I feel that I have a lot to offer. My work has been so highly praised that I feel it incumbent upon me to pass along something of benefit to the wanna-bes."

Good grief, she had nerve! I itched to throttle her on the spot. If I still had blood that could boil, this would do it. The thought that she might be going around masquerading as Dorinda, being this patronizing and conceited, infuriated me.

Dorinda continued, not having noticed the scowl on my face. "My books are transforming the genre, though I have to say, I don't really consider myself a *mystery* writer." Oh, the scorn that dripped from her voice as she spoke that word! "I read two or three mysteries before I started writing, and I realized that I could easily write something better and much more serious, even though I do use some of the conventions of the form."

I forced myself to take a step back from her. Otherwise, I was afraid that I might do something violent. What a load of pretentious tripe! This woman had to be stopped, and soon. I might have to sacrifice my anonymity to do it, but I couldn't allow her go around spouting such stupidity and besmirching my good name, as it were, as she did so.

"I'm sure I'll learn something from your talk," I said, though it was a wonder she could understand me, my teeth were clamped so hard together.

She smiled knowingly at me, then swept past me on her way into the dining room.

I stood there for a moment, fuming, trying hard to get a handle on my temper. I might end up smashing something—though that would in many ways be a mercy, considering the extreme tackiness of some of the so-called objets d'art gracing the halls of Kinsale House. That collection of garishly painted figures of the royal family on a nearby table might do for a start.

Had Giles not appeared just then, one or more of those ugly little statues might have been shattered. "Simon!" he said, coming up to me. "What's gotten your knickers in such a twist? You should see the expression on your face!"

Tersely I explained. Giles whistled. "What a cow! What are we going to do?"

"I'm going to that session and try to keep myself under control," I said, "and I have an assignment for you. I want you to cozy up to Lady Hermione's assistant, Mary Monkley, and find out what you can about this fake Dorinda. See if you can get a look, somehow, at any correspondence Lady Hermione might have exchanged with her. Get an address or something, if you can. I want to know who this woman is."

Giles sighed. "I think I'd rather go stake myself out on an anthill than have to chat up that little mouse. She'll probably faint when I get anywhere near her!"

"I think you underestimate your abilities to charm ladies of a certain age, Giles. Just bat those thick eyelashes of yours at her a few times and speak to

her soothingly in that plummy voice, and you'll
have her cooing in no time, no matter how timid
she is."

He did not seem to appreciate the levity in my
tone. "If you keep asking me to do such things,
Simon, I'll have to ask for a rise in salary." He
paused for a moment. "Or perhaps I'll have to insist on certain fringe benefits."

"Just do it," I said, ignoring the lascivious twist
of his lips. "I'll expect results from you before the
morning is over."

"Yes, sir!" Giles saluted and clicked his heels together. "Would you mind if I had some breakfast
first?"

I waved him away, and he pretended to stalk off.
Chuckling, my good humor restored, I headed upstairs to collect from my bedroom what I would
need for the morning sessions.

Ten minutes later I was downstairs again, finding a seat in the back of the room where the fake
Dorinda was scheduled to speak. As I waited, various conference attendees wandered in and sat down,
some of them chatting, others opening notebooks
and preparing to write down whatever words of wisdom Dorinda would have to offer.

Dorinda finally appeared, only about five minutes
late. She assumed a position in the front of the small
sitting room, which had been adapted for conference use by the addition of about twenty chairs
arranged in several short rows. Dorinda stood with
her back to a magnificent marble fireplace, fiddling with a sheaf of notes, which she placed on
the lectern in front of her.

She did nothing to introduce herself, other than
to mention her name and a couple of the titles of

the books *she* had written. I began to seethe. This was going to be every bit as trying as I had suspected.

It quickly got worse.

"I don't write mysteries," Dorinda announced. "I write novels in which unexplained deaths occur, and someone—namely, my heroine—has to figure out what happened. Because of that, I've been branded a mystery writer, and even my publisher puts the phrase 'a novel of suspense' on the covers of my books." She paused dramatically. "But what I write is serious fiction that just happens to be about crime and murder."

A hand shot up in the front row before she could expound further.

"Yes?" Dorinda said, her tone icy.

"Does this mean you're not going to tell us how to write a mystery novel?"

"If you'll be patient and listen to what I have to say," Dorinda replied, "you'll find out how to write *novels*. Just sit tight, and listen."

There was a bit of muttering after that comment, and not all of it came from me. Being rude to your audience isn't the best way to begin a lecture. Dorinda was digging the hole deeper and deeper every time she opened her mouth, and I was looking forward to pushing her into it and piling the dirt on top of her.

Dorinda stared down at her notes for a moment, then looked up and addressed her audience again. "No doubt you've all read my books, and you may have thought you knew what they were about. But now I'm going to analyze them for you and explain what was really going on in these books. I'm certain you'll understand better, once I've used the techniques of textual criticism on my work, and you'll see how what many have mistakenly identified as *genre* fiction is really something else entirely."

For a moment, I thought I might be trapped in an alternate universe. I had written what I thought were some darn good mysteries, what I thought were more than the garden variety whodunit. But the pretentious bullshit this fake Dorinda was spouting was nothing more than that: bullshit. Maybe this was what other writers experienced when they read articles or heard papers given on their work. On one level, it was fascinating to hear the "author's" interpretation of the work. But since I knew she hadn't written one single word of the books she was dissecting, it was plain old bullshit.

I stood it for as long as I could, listening to her rambling on and on about tropes and themes and other such literary folderol, and finally my temper got the better of me.

I stood up and interrupted her in full spate. "This is absolute nonsense, and you know it!"

"What? What on earth do you mean?" Dorinda paused, blinking. She had been so wrapped up in her mini-dissertation, it took her a moment to focus on what she had heard and just who was saying it.

I tried to choose my words with care. "Listening to this farrago of pretentiousness you're spouting, I'd say it's doubtful whether you really wrote these books."

Before Dorinda could respond, someone else spoke up. "I've read your books twice each, and I have to say, I didn't get any of what you've been talking about out of them."

I wanted to applaud the brave soul. I think.

"You don't know what you're talking about," Dorinda said huffily, "either of you." Then she focused on me. "Of course I wrote the books."

"Then why have you never made public appearances before now?" I asked her. "I know that you've never done an official signing for your books. Why now? Why are you now out in public, talking about your work?"

"I never felt the need before now," Dorinda said. "I thought the books would speak for themselves. But the more I read what others had to say about the books, and how mistaken they were, I decided I had to start getting out in public and talking about them, if they had any chance of being properly understood. This conference seemed like a good place to start."

"Maybe," I said, making those two syllables sound as insulting as I could. "But maybe you're impersonating the real author, who chooses to remain anonymous. Maybe you're an opportunist, and you're hoping to get attention by pulling a stunt like this."

Heads swiveled back and forth between Dorinda and me, waiting for the next fusillade.

"I don't know who the bloody hell you think you are," Dorinda said, her voice rising, "and I don't know why you should be trying to vilify and persecute me in this strange manner. If you persist in this, I shall have no choice but to ask my lawyers to take action against you."

"Oh, really?" I said. This had actually started to turn funny. "And what would your so-called lawyers say when they find out you're not really who you say you are? Don't you think they'll be a bit miffed with you?"

"Why? *Why* are you doing this?" Dorinda wailed, then burst into tears.

Accusing eyes turned toward me as the audience watched for my response. It was apparently one thing to argue with the woman, and another to have made her cry.

"Because," I responded, "you are deliberately misrepresenting the work of the author who is really Dorinda Darlington. I know Dorinda, and I know that you're an impostor."

A collective gasp rose from the conference attendees, and almost as one, their heads swiveled back toward Dorinda. How would she respond to such a direct accusation?

The tears dried abruptly. "Well, Mr. Know-it-all, if I'm not Dorinda Darlington, who is?"

"The *real* Dorinda prefers to preserve her anonymity."

"How convenient for you!"

"Why are you persisting in this charade?"

"*You* are the only one who insists it's a charade!" She stamped her foot in frustration.

"Don't worry," I said, oozing false sympathy as I spoke. "This will all soon be over. Dorinda's agent will be here later today, and I'm sure she'll be happy to verify the fact that you're an impostor."

More muttering filled the room as the fascinated group chewed over this bit of information.

I felt a strong wave of hate emanating from the fake Dorinda. Frankly, I was surprised she hadn't given up by now and fled the room, shedding more of the crocodile tears she had produced just moments ago.

"That's just fine with me," she said. "I welcome the chance to be vindicated."

"You're totally off your rocker," I said hotly. "You're a fake, and you know it. Why don't you confess now and just end this travesty?"

"I'll see you in hell first," she said. She snatched up her papers and stalked from the room.

Chapter Eight

My temper is one of the vestiges of the human being I once was, and from time to time I still have difficulty controlling it. Most of the time, I'm really rather easygoing.

Once the fake Dorinda had left the room, the conference attendees shifted uneasily in their chairs and started muttering. I had been more aggressive than I had intended in winding the impostor up, and I had probably tipped my hand a bit too early in the game. So be it.

Now I figured I'd better deal with the situation I had just created. I stood up and walked to the front of the room. I waited for the muttering to die down; then I spoke.

"My apologies to everyone for the little scene I just caused, but I'm sure you will all understand, as writers yourselves, that I take the matter of intellectual theft very seriously indeed." Here I paused for the vigorous nods of assent and the assorted "Certainly!"

"This matter will be sorted out, and at some point, no doubt, you'll hear more about it," I said, though I didn't intend to bring the real Dorinda totally out of the closet, as it were. "For the time remaining in this session, perhaps you'll permit *me* to talk about the works of Dorinda Darlington. I have read them all, and I do admire them. I'd love to share with you my own thoughts about these books." I smiled modestly.

Detecting no dissent from my proposal, I launched into a brief discussion of the structure of my mystery novels, giving the group pointers for plotting, creating characters, and so on. I believe I can say with no exaggeration whatsoever that it was a far more useful, not to say truthful, talk than what the fake Dorinda had been shoveling on them.

I was just about to answer a question when Lady Hermione sailed into the room and accosted me. "Dr. Kirby-Jones! A word with you, if you please!"

Everyone in the room jumped along with me.

"Of course, Lady Hermione. I believe we've finished here. I'll be happy to answer questions later on, so please do let me know if there's anything else I can answer for you." I smiled at the group, and they applauded as I followed Lady Hermione from the room.

I could tell from the tone of Lady Hermione's voice that something had aroused her ire, and I feared it was my behavior with the faux Dorinda. I was sure she had wasted no time in going to tattle, and by the set of Lady Hermione's shoulders, I was in for quite a dressing-down. I smiled. Lady Hermione had a surprise or two in store.

My hostess said nothing further until we arrived in her drawing room, where Dorinda sat calmly on a chair, pouring herself a cup of tea.

Lady Hermione pointed toward a chair, clearly ordering me to take a seat. I ignored her. With eyes narrowed, Lady Hermione sat and glared up at me.

I waited.

"What is this preposterous allegation of yours, Dr. Kirby-Jones? How dare you disrupt the proceedings of this conference with such a taradiddle!"

Before Lady Hermione could draw breath to launch further into her tirade, I interposed loudly, "The 'taradiddle,' as you so quaintly put it, is the pack of lies this woman, whoever she is, has handed you. She is *not* Dorinda Darlington, and I am well able to back up my accusation, I can assure you."

Lady Hermione blinked. I rather doubted anyone, her whole life, had spoken back to her in such a commanding tone. Apparently, when a peasant has the nerve to revolt, it quite oversets the aristocracy.

"You see, now, Lady Hermione, what I was talking about," Dorinda crowed. "What an absolute jerk this man is, and how unbelievably nasty? How he has the nerve to stand there and talk to you, of all people, in that rude manner, well . . ." Her voice trailed off as Lady Hermione trained a gimlet eye upon her.

"How do you know that this woman *isn't* Dorinda Darlington, Dr. Kirby-Jones?" Lady Hermione voiced her question in what was, for her, a mild tone.

"Because, my dear Lady Hermione," I said, making my own timbre as soothing and conciliatory as possible, "the *real* Dorinda is a close friend of mine, and I know how appalled she would be to discover someone masquerading as her. And, moreover, doing it so shabbily."

The fake started to sputter at that, but our hostess held up a hand to shush her.

"Then who is the *real* Dorinda, Dr. Kirby-Jones?" Lady Hermione asked.

I held up my hands in a placatory manner. "I'm afraid, dear lady, that I am not at liberty to divulge that information. Dorinda guards her privacy most jealously, you see. She is of a rather retiring nature and prefers to let her work speak for itself."

"This is most unsatisfactory." Lady Hermione frowned, but I could see that doubt had already taken root. The waves of irritation emanating from her spoke volumes. Things did not bode well for faux Dorinda.

I smiled. "I can well understand your position, Lady Hermione, and indeed I sympathize with you. You had no reason to suspect that an impostor had taken advantage of your celebrated reputation in order to play some devious game of her own." Said impostor began sputtering again, so I raised my voice to drown her out. "But when Nina Yaknova arrives, she will be able to settle this matter once and for all. Nina knows the real Dorinda, and I have no doubt that she will put paid to this woman's little act."

Lady Hermione took a deep breath and sat back, her head going slowly back and forth between me and That Woman, as I was now beginning to think of her. I kept quiet, waiting.

"By all means, let us wait until Nina is here." Lady Hermione stood up as she spoke. "Until that time, however, I believe I will ask you, Miss Darlington, or whoever you may be, not to have any further contact with the conference attendees. That shouldn't be long, as I expect Nina will arrive from London in time for our tea break this afternoon. Then we shall clear up this matter completely, and one of you will be asked to leave."

Eyes blazing, That Woman stood up. "Well, it shan't be I! Because if I am forced to leave, you won't be the only one to regret it, Lady Hermione! You can lay odds on that. If I'm forced to leave, someone's going to pay, and pay dearly." She displayed her teeth in a most vulpine manner. "But if I'm forced to leave, I suppose I shall just go off to Brighton and spend a few days at the Marston Arms. I've heard it's a lovely, secluded sort of place. Perfect for getting away from prying eyes."

The effect of these last few sentences upon Lady Hermione was astounding. The blood drained from her face, her mouth fell open, and she collapsed slowly down into her chair. That Woman laughed before marching out of the room, head held high.

"My dear Lady Hermione, are you all right?" I approached her and went down on one knee. She almost literally stank of fear, and I thought she might be having a heart attack.

"Brandy," Lady Hermione muttered, waving a hand vaguely in the direction of a drinks tray nearby. "Some brandy, please."

Quickly I fetched her a healthy tot of brandy, and as she sipped it, the color came gradually back to her face.

"Thank you, Dr. Kirby-Jones," she said, her voice weak. "I'm afraid that you've discovered one of my little secrets. I do have a bit of a heart condition, and nasty scenes like that do sometimes cause me a bad moment or two. But I shall be quite all right in a few moments."

She couldn't look me in the eyes as she said that. I knew very well that her shock stemmed from the mention of that hotel in Brighton, rather than the unpleasant confrontation with That Woman, but I wasn't going to risk another episode of heart palpitations to pry the truth out of her. At least, not right this minute.

Lady Hermione was obviously hiding something. Did That Woman really know what it was, or was she bluffing? And could she use it as leverage with Lady Hermione against me?

I continued to watch my hostess with concern. Though she seemed to have regained her composure, I thought she was still a bit shaky. Nevertheless, trying to appear as if nothing untoward had happened, she rose from her chair.

"Thank you, Dr. Kirby-Jones. I feel quite restored. Now, if you will excuse me, I must see how everyone is getting on. I shall expect you here again for tea. Until then, I would be greatly indebted to you if you would forbear to mention any of this to your fellow guests." The appeal in her eyes was unmistakable.

"Certainly, Lady Hermione," I murmured. "I am at your disposal."

I watched her depart and pondered what I should do next. I wasn't scheduled to speak for another hour yet.

"That was quite an interesting scene, don't you think?"

I started in surprise. The voice had come from somewhere behind me. I turned. Dexter Harbaugh's head rose, seemingly disembodied, over the edge of a couch that faced one of the windows in a corner of the room.

"How long have you been there?" I asked. A

rather pointless question, obviously, since he had to have been there all along.

Harbaugh got up from the couch and stood, blinking and yawning. I waited.

He ignored my question. "Didn't mean to nod off, but the bed in my room is damned uncomfortable. Thought a little kip here would be just the thing while Dragon Lady was off on her rounds."

"Didn't you have a session this morning?" I had glanced over the schedule earlier, and I was pretty sure that Harbaugh was to have given a workshop this morning.

He snorted. "I gave them a writing assignment. I'm not going to stand there and blather at them. They're writers—or think they are, anyway. They might as well write."

"Good point. But then you'll have to read their assignments and comment on them."

"No. They'll do it for one another. Not me. Do you think I'm bloody stupid?" He grinned. "You might have come here to work, but I didn't."

"Silly me," I said dryly.

"You've certainly managed to liven things up for this week," Harbaugh said, his tone almost admiring. "And here was I, thinking this was going to be just another bloody boring week at Kinsale House. Trust a drama queen to stir things up."

I decided to ignore the sneer in his voice and on his face. "I'm not the one misrepresenting myself." Well, not completely, anyway.

"Wonder what her game is," Harbaugh mused, suddenly making a beeline for the drinks tray. He poured himself a stiff shot of whisky and downed it in one gulp. He filled the glass again, but this time let the whisky linger on his tongue long enough that he could actually taste it.

"I suppose we'll find out at some point," I responded. "Had you ever met this woman before?"

He set the glass down on the tray with a slight thump. "Have I ever met Dorinda Darlington before? No, can't say as I ever had the pleasure." He headed past me, toward the door. "Now, if you'll excuse me, I'd better go check in on my little band of wanna-bes."

I don't suppose he thought I was smart enough to realize he hadn't answered my question.

This situation was getting more interesting by the moment. What did Dexter Harbaugh know about That Woman? And why was he not admitting he knew her?

Chapter Nine

"**R**aymond Chandler once wrote that when he got stuck for something to do to advance the plot, he had a man come through the door with a gun."

I paused for the chuckles this line invariably brought.

"Of course, if you're writing a novel set in the tenth century, this won't work."

There were a few more chuckles at this one, but, amazingly, a hand shot up in the back of the room.

"Why not, Dr. Kirby-Jones?"

I examined the questioner closely. About twenty, he appeared genuinely puzzled at the snickers that greeted his query. After a moment's further study, I concluded he was serious. He genuinely didn't understand.

"Because guns hadn't been invented in the tenth century." I tried to keep my tone noncommittal.

After all, I had told them at the beginning of my talk that there were no stupid questions, that they should feel free to ask anything. But I had supposed—wrongly, it now appeared—that anyone interested in writing historical fiction would have a basic acquaintance with some facts of history. I peered across the room at his name badge. *Geoff Monkley* was scrawled in bold lettering. Could he be related to Lady Hermione's assistant, Mary Monkley?

As the sounds of mirth subsided, I continued. "If you're going to write in the genre known as 'alternate history,' you can play with the facts of history and introduce anachronisms deliberately." I could see that Geoff had no idea what an anachronism was and now was too embarrassed to ask. "An anachronism is the placing of a person, place, event, or object in the incorrect historical period. For example, like having Moses print out the Ten Commandments on his laser printer." I got some guffaws with that one.

Geoff's face cleared. Now he understood me. "If you're going to write straight historical fiction or historical mysteries, rather than alternate history or historical fantasy, then you should stick to the facts as closely as possible. When you deviate from them, you'd better have a darn good reason and be willing to explain it to your readers. Nothing will ruin a book faster for an intelligent reader than inaccuracies. They might slip by a lot of readers, but inevitably, there will be at least one person who will catch you out."

That touched off a lively debate, and thus I kept my group of conference-goers busy for another half hour. By the end of the session, I was exhilarated. I patted myself on the back—metaphorically, that is—for having given them their many pounds' worth. I had been horrified—and fascinated—when I discovered just how much Lady Hermione charged them for this week, and was therefore all the more determined to ensure that they got something out of it, at least from me.

As usual, there were one or two who lingered behind to ask further questions after the rest had headed off thirstily for their tea. Thus it was that I arrived in Lady Hermione's drawing room for my own tea a bit later than the rest of my fellow conference speakers.

Many of our tea breaks were communal, giving us opportunities to spend time informally with our students. Lady Hermione had arranged one meeting each day, though, for just the speakers. Her way, I suppose, of keeping tabs on what transpired each day. This session promised to be of particular interest, given my confrontations with the faux Dorinda earlier in the day.

All heads turned in my direction as I entered the room, as if they had been waiting impatiently for my arrival. I scanned the room quickly. Nina Yaknova had not yet arrived, it seemed. Where was the dratted woman? Late, as usual.

With her hands clenched tightly in her lap, That Woman sat in a chair near the center of the room, not far from Lady Hermione and her shadow, Mary Monkley. Miss Monkley was scribbling industriously in a notebook as Lady Hermione issued instructions for some adjustments to tomorrow's schedule of workshops.

Patty Anne Putney, beaming with goodwill and stroking Mr. Murbles constantly, approached me. I plastered a welcoming smile on my face.

"Mr. Murbles is so pleased with you, Dr. Kirby-

Jones," Patty Anne said, leaning close and whispering in the general direction of my left ear.

"And why is that?" I asked politely, eyeing the bunny dubiously.

"He heard that you put that dreadful woman in her place," she responded, and one hand manipulated Mr. Murbles's head, so that it seemed he was nodding in approbation at me.

"Delighted, I'm sure," I said. She appeared unaffected by the tinge of sarcasm in my tone.

"Can you believe," she whispered indignantly, "that dreadful woman had the nerve to tell Mr. Murbles our books are saccharine enough to send a diabetic into shock? How could she say something so hurtful to Mr. Murbles? Miss Edwina Aiken and Hodge are beloved by millions of readers, and that woman would do well to remember not everyone wants to read about a heroine like hers."

The disdain in her voice caught me by surprise. "Why? What's wrong with her?"

Patty Anne's eyes widened in horror. "She smokes!"

I nodded, still perplexed.

"That's not very ladylike, is it?" Patty Anne hissed at me, clearly pleased at having made her point.

If this woman's balloon ever landed, I wanted to be present to see it.

"But apparently she didn't write those books after all," she continued. "Dreadful woman! Mr. Murbles doesn't like her, not at all. He thinks she should be asked to leave Kinsale House immediately."

"It won't be long now before that happens," I assured her. "As soon as Nina Yaknova arrives, the game will be up."

Miss Putney drew back in horror. "Is *she* coming here?"

"Do you mean Nina?" I asked. "Yes, didn't you see her name listed on your schedule?"

She shook her head violently. "No! Mr. Murbles and I wouldn't be here at all if we knew *she* was going to be here." Her grip on Mr. Murbles had tightened to the point that the poor bunny appeared to be choking.

"Is Nina your agent?" I asked, fascinated.

"She used to be," Miss Putney hissed. "Before Mr. Murbles and I caught on to her vicious ways. She is *not* a lady! And she does *not* conduct herself in a way remotely becoming to one."

Right on cue, Nina stormed in, Giles trailing in her wake and frowning mightily.

"Hermione, my dear, how are you?" Nina asked. She came to a halt in front of our hostess and waited, foot tapping, as Lady Hermione rose, then bent down to exchange air kisses with her. Conversation around us had ceased completely in anticipation of the fireworks.

"I'm delighted you finally managed to arrive, Nina," Lady Hermione said. "We've been expecting you."

They eyed each other as adversaries in the ring often do. I expected them to start circling any moment now, looking for a vulnerable spot for the knockout punch. Lady Hermione had the advantages of her superior height and breeding. Nina simply fought dirty.

"One does have a business to run, after all, Hermione," Nina observed. "I couldn't tell the prime minister to call back, just because talking to him would make me late for dear Lady Hermione's little afternoon tea, now, could I?"

Lady Hermione's lips tightened. Knowing Nina

as I did, I doubted she was bluffing. Lady Hermione knew it, too.

"I'm sure you're to be congratulated, Nina, on having signed the prime minister as a client. But I have a more pressing concern at the moment."

"Thank you, Hermione. Now whatever is the matter? Has one of your little pets written a best-seller?" I could have smacked Nina myself for the patronizing air with which she delivered that last line.

Nina turned to Giles. "Tea, please. Black, two lumps."

To his credit, Giles bit back a retort—no doubt about the lumps he would like to give her—and went to get her a cup of tea from the nearby cart. I would have a few choice words for her later on her manners—or rather, her lack of them.

"Now, you were saying . . . ?" Nina affected a bored tone as she turned back to Lady Hermione. Giles had handed her a cup of tea, and she stirred it.

"There is a bit of a dispute we're hoping that you can resolve, Nina," Lady Hermione said, her voice remarkably controlled. "Professor Kirby-Jones claims that one amongst us is an impostor."

"Simon, what on earth are you playing at?" Setting down her tea without having tasted it, Nina turned toward me. "Stirring up a little drama, are we?"

"I suppose one could look at it that way, Nina, dearest," I said, taking a few strides to stand beside her and looking down upon her gamine face. "Someone here is claiming to be one of your clients. Dorinda Darlington, in fact."

Nina's eyes flickered. She turned away from me and picked up her tea. As I watched, she walked over to where the faux Dorinda sat on a couch, and seated herself beside the impostor. She set down her cup of tea on the table in front of the couch.

"But, Simon, darling, you know Dorinda is one of my clients. There's no pretense involved in that."

The patronizing tone nettled me. She'd never before spoken to me in such fashion. "I know that, Nina, darling. Forgive me for being imprecise. Someone is here claiming to be Dorinda Darlington." As if she didn't know this already, from our conversation several days ago in her office.

"Really, Simon? How terribly interesting." Nina couldn't have looked more bored. "Who, pray tell?"

With a sweep of my hand, I indicated the woman sitting beside her. Nina picked up her tea and took a sip before placing the cup back on the table.

"Hello, Dorinda, dearest," Nina cooed. "Is Simon playing naughty games again?"

Chapter Ten

———— ☠ ————

Treachery, thy name is Nina!

I was relieved to find that I had not spoken those words aloud. In fact, for once in my death, I had been struck speechless.

One could have heard the proverbial pin drop in the room after Nina's words of greeting to That Woman. Then came a collective intake of breath before gabbling broke out all over the room. I was almost dizzy from the assault of words coming from all around me.

Nina had severely damaged my credibility. Lady Hermione now eyed me as if I were something just retrieved from the nearest rubbish tip. How on earth was I to respond to this, other than by outing myself as the real Dorinda Darlington? If I did, who would believe me now that Nina had spoken?

I made two quick decisions. The first was that I would find myself a new agent forthwith. Hitting

Nina in the pocketbook was the only kind of threat she'd understand. Fortunately for me, I had nothing new under contract via Nina, so I was free to shop around for agents.

The second decision was that I would go along with Nina for the moment. She was playing some sort of deep game. I doubted it would be to my advantage, one way or another, but I'd hold my tongue and see how this all played out.

"Dr. Kirby-Jones!"

Lady Hermione rattled the rafters, as usual.

"Have you been playing some sort of game with us and baiting this poor young woman?" Lady Hermione's expression boded nothing but ill for yours truly.

"No, Hermione, he has not!"

Isabella Veryan's sudden defense of me was quite a surprise. I turned to look at her in astonishment.

Lady Hermione appeared just as startled as I. "Belle! What do you mean? What do you know about this?"

Isabella came to stand beside me, placing a reassuring hand on my arm. "I've not known Simon all that long, Hermione, but I'm an excellent judge of character, and if he says that woman is an impostor, then I believe him." She tossed her head in the direction of Nina and Dorinda. "Moreover, that viper would swear the sun was shining in the midst of a torrential downpour if it suited her purposes."

Oh ho, I thought. *Bad blood between Isabella and Nina. Who would have thought it?*

"Dear Isabella, so forthright as always." Nina's voice slid lazily forth, like the hiss of the viper Isabella had called her. "I had forgotten how dearly you love to hold on to a grudge, no matter how misguided."

"That's doing it up a bit brown, Nina." George

Austen-Hare had entered the fray. Now I had him on one side of me and Dame Isabella on the other. "We all know what you did to Isabella over the rights to her backlist when she changed publishers. Nothing short of criminal, that was. No wonder she left you. Bloody piracy, that's what it was!"

I had had no idea Isabella was no longer a client of Nina's. Nina certainly hadn't advertised that fact; it must be a fairly recent development.

Nina's eyes narrowed at George's barb, and I thought for a moment she would come off the sofa and attack poor George with her bare hands. Instead, she settled for something deadlier.

"Ah, George, George," she cooed. "I truly am delighted that you're still able to peddle your male sex fantasies under the guise of romantic suspense. I didn't mind the money, frankly, but your feeble attempts at getting me in bed were more than I could bear. I hear you don't have that problem with your current agent." Her mouth twisted in a moue of distaste. "The poor dear must be truly *desperate* for clients to have to stoop so low."

I could feel the sheer rage boiling within poor Austen-Hare. I couldn't blame him. I had seen Nina nasty before, but nothing to compare with this. She was begging to be murdered, and I wouldn't be surprised if someone obliged at the rate she was going.

I had also had no idea that George Austen-Hare had defected, along with Isabella Veryan. No wonder Nina was so thrilled to have Ashford Dunn signed up now.

"Oh, come on, man," Dexter Harbaugh spoke up. "Slap the silly bitch, and be done with it." He knocked back the rest of his drink, set his glass down upon a table, and ambled over to stand in front of George,

Isabella, and me, facing Nina. "She just needs a little knocking around. Show her who's boss. She works for us, after all. Where would she be without writers?"

"Don't be ridiculous, Dexter," George snapped. "I've never struck a woman, not even one who tries to provoke me in such a vulgar manner."

"Yes, Dexter, don't be ridiculous," Nina said, her voice hard. "If you had the balls to actually strike a woman, you wouldn't write about it so lovingly in your books. Talk about living vicariously!" She began laughing uproariously.

Dexter Harbaugh's back went rigid. Like George moments before, he simmered with rage. Taking a step forward, he picked up Nina's cup of tea from the table and dashed its contents into her face. Nina stopped laughing and started yowling.

Dorinda screamed and jumped up from the couch. "You animal! You could have blinded her!" Before anyone realized what she was doing, she stepped around the table and laid into Dexter Harbaugh with one slap after another. Harbaugh was too dazed at first to respond. Then his fists started flailing back at her. It took Giles and me several moments to get the two of them separated.

"Enough!" Lady Hermione bellowed, and I'd swear that all of Kinsale House shook as if it had been hit by an earthquake.

"This is an utter disgrace!" Thankfully, Lady Hermione dropped her decibel level considerably. "I am appalled—utterly and entirely appalled—by your behavior. All of you!" She paused. She was so angry her chest was heaving with the exertion of breathing.

"Dr. Kirby-Jones, Nina, I want the two of you to stay. The rest of you are dismissed, for the moment.

Go to your rooms, and consider what you've said and done here. I will speak to each of you, after I have decided whether to continue with this week's conference."

The whole roomful of people had frozen into place.

"Dismissed!" Lady Hermione barked again. Mary Monkley cowered behind her. Patty Anne Putney took Dexter Harbaugh by the arm, murmuring in his ear—soothingly, no doubt—while Mr. Murbles remained his imperturbable self. They led him out of the room. Isabella Veryan and George Austen-Hare strode arm in arm behind them, with Norah Tattersall trailing in their wake. Ashford Dunn, who had hovered silently near Nina during the fore-going fracas, lingered at the doorway, gazing back and forth from Nina to the fake Dorinda.

"I think perhaps I should be here, too, Lady Her-mione," That Woman said, her voice quavering.

"I think not," Lady Hermione said.

"Come on," Ashford Dunn said, grabbing at Do-rinda's arm. "Idiot!" he hissed at her in an under-tone. I could hear him, but I doubted either Nina or Lady Hermione could. "You'll ruin everything. Come on!"

Dorinda stood, wavering, but Ashford Dunn took hold of her and pulled her from the room.

Now only Nina and I were left in the room with our irate hostess.

Nina had wiped the tea from her eyes and face, though her eyes continued to stream with tears.

"Dr. Kirby-Jones," Lady Hermione addressed me in a calmer tone, "do you have any amendment to your accusation?"

I shook my head. "No, Lady Hermione. I still maintain that the woman claiming to be Dorinda

Darlington is an impostor. I am prepared, if necessary, to prove it beyond a shadow of a doubt."

"Nina, do you have anything you would like to say?"

"No, Hermione, dear, I have nothing to add." Nina affected nonchalance, but I knew she was doing a masterful job of concealing her anger.

"I will get to the bottom of this," Lady Hermione vowed, "and whichever of you is lying to me will regret it. Have no doubt of that." She drew a deep breath. "Now, if you will be so kind as to leave me." She turned to her secretary. "Brandy, Mary, if you please."

As Mary Monkley scurried to fulfill her employer's bidding, Lady Hermione leaned back in her chair and closed her eyes. Her face had turned ashen, and I wondered whether calling a doctor might be in order. Now, however, would not be the moment to suggest that, I decided. I left her to the tender mercies of Mary Monkley.

Neither Nina nor I said a word as we left the room. Once I had closed the door behind us, however, I caught Nina's arm and spun her around to face me.

"What the hell was all that about, Nina? What's going on here?"

Ashford Dunn chose that moment to erupt from somewhere nearby. "Take your hands off her!"

"Call off your boy toy, Nina, and answer my question." I stared at the two of them. Dunn had wrapped an arm protectively around Nina's padded shoulders, while Nina smirked at me.

"You don't have to pay any attention to him, Nina." Dunn glared daggers at me.

My own knight-errant made his entrance upon that cue. "Oh, come off it, barrow boy." The withering contempt in Giles's voice made Dunn blanch, even though he probably hadn't a clue as to what Giles meant by that derogatory term. "The woman obviously has bigger balls than you do. I doubt she really needs some jumped-up johnny from the cornfields of Iowa to fight her battles for her."

"Now it's your *boy toy* to the rescue, Simon." Nina laughed. "And here I thought he was just good for fetching tea, eh, Giles?"

"That's *Sir* Giles to you and your little gutter-snipe." Normally Giles eschews his lord-of-the-manor status—after all, he's a mere baronet—but when he wants to, he can sound intolerably upper crust.

"Oh, my," Nina said, unimpressed. "*Sir* Boy Toy. Lah-di-da."

Giles wasn't fazed. "You're so good at sticking knives in other people's backs, it's a pity someone hasn't performed the same service for you."

Nina laughed. "Dear me, it has teeth. And it can bite. Oh, I'm terrified."

All this time, Dunn had been fuming silently. "I ought to thrash you, you upper-class poof!" I wonder how long it had taken him to come up with something that breathtakingly trite.

"Save your energy for Nina's bedroom." Giles refused to be drawn.

"Enough!" I said, though I had actually been rather amused by their little catfight—amused enough that my own temper had cooled a bit. "I'm still waiting for an explanation, Nina. What's going on here?"

"Now, Simon, that would be telling, wouldn't it?" Nina batted her eyes flirtatiously at me, and I could feel Giles tensing beside me. "You'll just have to trust me, won't you?"

"Unfortunately, I don't think I can."

"You really have no choice." Nina dropped the

casual manner. She shook off Ashford Dunn's arm, startling him. "I'm going out on the terrace for a smoke, since Hermione has the fits if anyone smokes inside Kinsale House. I'll talk to you later, Simon." She turned to Dunn for a moment. "Ash, dear, we'll talk about your new contract later. Now, why don't you go upstairs and get some work done on your new book? That deadline is coming up, and we wouldn't want to miss it, now, would we?"

"Yes, Nina," Dunn said docilely. No doubt about who held the reins there. He headed for the stairs, pausing long enough to direct a baleful stare in Giles's direction. Nina, without a backward glance, walked down the hallway and through a door. I hadn't yet seen the terrace at Kinsale House, but presumably, Nina knew how to find it. I noted the door through which she had gone; I'd go after her in a few minutes.

"What are you going to do, Simon? What the hell is she playing at, do you think?" Giles turned to me, his handsome brow furrowed in irritation.

"I'm not sure what's going on, Giles," I said, "but you can bet I'm going to get to the bottom of it. Nina's devious, which it didn't take me long to discover. That's probably a good quality for an agent to have, especially one as high-powered as Nina. But I hadn't expected this level of duplicity."

"She's a nasty piece of work."

"Yes, and I'm beginning to see just how nasty she can be." I frowned. "Maybe this is some kind of publicity stunt on her part, but I can't figure out what the point is, if it's intended for publicity's sake."

"She has obviously treated some of the other writers here rather shabbily."

"Yes, she's made several enemies; that much is evident. I wouldn't be alone, dancing on her grave."

Giles laughed at that. "No, I'm sure there'd be quite a party."

"Would you mind, Giles," I asked him, "running up to fetch my sunglasses and a hat for me? I'm going to track Nina down on that terrace and try to force her to talk to me."

"No need, Simon," Giles said, "though you know I'd not mind in the least." His eyes slid away from mine for a moment. "I was just out for a brief walk. The sky is quite dark. If it hasn't started raining yet, it won't be long, by the looks of things." I've told him I have a slight allergy to sunlight, which is true, of course, but he doesn't know quite why I'm allergic.

"Then I'd better try to track Nina down before we both get wet," I said. "Any progress with your inquiries?"

"I'm compiling quite a lot of information," Giles said. "I'll have plenty for you to dig through by this evening."

"Good," I said. "Keep at it." I strode off down the hall, toward the door through which Nina had disappeared.

I found myself in yet another sitting room, this one furnished in true Pukka Sahib. The large chamber bulged with various artifacts, most of them in questionable taste, from the Indian subcontinent. What is it with the British and elephants' feet? I shuddered and averted my eyes as I approached French windows on the other side of the room.

One of the windows stood slightly ajar, and I pulled it open and stepped out onto the terrace. As Giles had said, the sky was dark and gray. Though it was not yet raining, I doubted it would be long before it poured.

The terrace was a broad expanse of worn and aged stone, probably twenty-five feet by twenty, I estimated. Midway there, I espied Nina, sitting at a small table and smoking.

I hastened toward her, anxious to question her further. "Nina! I want to talk to you!"

Nina looked toward me and tilted her head to one side. She took a long drag from her cigarette and expelled smoke as she stood up. She walked away from me, toward the balustrade and the steps that lead down to a broad expanse of lawn. As she reached the balustrade, she leaned over to pitch her fag end onto the lawn.

I was by this time only a few feet from her, and her shrill screams stopped me in my tracks.

"Nina! What on earth is it?"

The cigarette butt still smoldering in her fingers, Nina turned to face me, all color drained from her face. "My God!" she said. "They've bloody well killed her!"

Chapter Eleven

"What?" I rushed over to Nina and looked down over the stone balustrade to see a body sprawled below, half in and half out of a flower bed. A stone urn had mashed the head like a melon dropped on concrete. I quickly averted my gaze from the pulpy mass. It was Dorinda; I recognized her from her clothes. She was as dead as the proverbial doornail. No need to go down there and muck about in the mess of her death; I could feel her death from here. It's a vampire thing, you know; if I focus, I can feel and almost hear someone else's heartbeat. The fake Dorinda's heart had stopped beating.

I turned back to Nina, whose eyes were still glazed over from the shock of her discovery. She was mumbling to herself, but I could make out the words with little difficulty. "Can't believe they actually did it! Why on earth? The stupid bitch! What did she do?"

"Nina! Get a grip!" I clasped one of her hands in mine. It was even colder than my own.

Taking a deep breath to steady herself, Nina focused on me. She withdrew her hand from mine, then pulled another cigarette from her purse. Her hands were almost steady as she lighted the cigarette.

"What did you mean by 'they,' Nina? Who was responsible for this?"

Nina blew smoke in my face. "I was just shocked, Simon. If anyone's responsible, it was probably that snotty boyfriend of yours!"

She had begun to recover; the barracuda was back.

Now was not the time to convince Nina that Giles was not my boyfriend. "Don't be ridiculous, Nina! Giles would not have killed this woman. He had no reason for doing such a thing."

Nina tossed her head. "Come off it, Simon! Anyone can see the idiot is besotted with you. Who's to say he didn't do it, thinking it was in your best interests?"

Ignoring my sputtered protests, Nina pointed to her left. "The urn used to sit on there, on the balustrade. Dorinda must have been standing on the lawn beneath, and someone pushed it off on her."

"Yes, it certainly looks that way."

Nina exhaled a cloud of smoke. She extracted a mobile phone from her purse. "Here." She handed it to me. "Summon someone."

I recalled from memory the number of our local crack homicide specialist, Detective Inspector Robin

Chase, and punched it in on the keypad. Robin was in his office, and I tersely explained what had happened. To his credit, Robin made no comment on my reporting yet another corpse. Instead, he assured me that he and a team from CID would soon be here at Kinsale House to take charge.

I handed Nina's mobile back to her and informed her that the authorities were on the way. Then I took her arm and guided her away from the scene of the crime. "I think we'd better go inside now." I looked up into the sky. Rain was imminent. "And I think I'd better find something to throw over the body before the rain washes everything away."

Nina grimaced. "I believe I shall leave that little detail to you, Simon."

"Yes, heaven forfend that you should get *your* hands grubby, dear Nina." She ignored that as I ushered her back into the house, into the Raj Room, as I had decided to call it.

"Did you see anything before I joined you, Nina? Anything that the police should know?"

She faced me, her chin set with determination. "Don't be ridiculous, Simon. What could I have seen? She must have already been dead when I went out onto the terrace."

She didn't exactly answer my question, but now was not the time to pin her down. Later on I'd tackle her about who or what she might have seen on the terrace. She might actually have seen the murderer leaving the scene of the crime, but Nina wouldn't part with that information until she had figured out how best to use it to her own advantage.

"We'll continue this later, but for now, go find Lady Hermione and break the news to her." I glanced around the room. Several hideous tiger-skin rugs littered the floor. I gathered up three of them, while Nina marched huffily out of the room.

Out on the terrace, I quickly shook out as much dust as I could from the tiger skins, then went and placed them across the corpse and as much of the crime scene as I could. Rain began to pelt down as I was placing the last tiger skin, and I hoped that Robin and his team would get here soon, in time to protect the area more effectively.

I sprinted back inside and shut the French windows firmly behind me. I realized too late that I shouldn't have touched the handles again. Now I would have smeared the fingerprints someone else might have left on them. Wiping the rain away from my face and head with my handkerchief, I looked up to see Lady Hermione come charging through the door from the hall.

"Dr. Kirby-Jones! Whatever is going on here? Nina said you had found Miss Darlington dead on the lawn!"

She had continued toward me as she spoke, and as she made a move to go past me, to open the doors out onto the terrace, I laid a restraining hand on her arm. She stiffened.

"Pardon me, Lady Hermione, but your getting wet and looking at what happened will serve no purpose right now. We've summoned the police, and it's best now to wait until they arrive." She made a move to shrug off my hand, and I applied gentle pressure. "Please, Lady Hermione, don't go out there."

"Very well," she said, suddenly yielding. "No doubt you're right. There's nothing I can do, I suppose. You're entirely certain the poor girl is . . . dead?" She faced me with horror dawning in her eyes.

"Yes, I'm sure." I resisted any urge to tell her just how well I knew death. I doubted it would have been of any comfort.

"Poor girl," she repeated. "Nothing like this has ever happened at Kinsale House."

I didn't take that as an accusation, though it had sounded a bit like one. "I know this is terribly upsetting, Lady Hermione, but I'm sure the police will soon find out what happened. I know the officer who will no doubt be in charge of the investigation, and he is highly competent. He'll get this sorted out in no time."

Lady Hermione's eyes narrowed as she examined me. "Ah, yes," she said, her tone cool. "You do have firsthand experience with murder, don't you? The late, unlamented postmistress of Snupperton Mumsley." She sniffed. "One had quite forgotten that."*

At this rate, I doubted I'd ever be on the guest list for Kinsale House again. Oh, well, at least I wouldn't have to be offended by the dubious taste of generations of Kinsales and their misguided attempts at decoration.

"Perhaps we should await the arrival of the police in your sitting room," I suggested. Lady Hermione sniffed once before stalking out of the room, leaving me to follow or not.

I followed.

Nina was ensconced in a chair, calmly sipping tea, when Lady Hermione and I arrived in the sitting room. Lady Hermione poured herself another stiff tot of brandy, tossed it down, then rang the bell. Dingleby appeared moments later, as if he had been hovering in the hall outside.

---

* Recounted in *Posted to Death*.

"Yes, Lady Hermione?"

"More tea, Dingleby. The police will be arriving shortly. One of our guests has met with an unfortunate accident on the terrace. When the police arrive, be so good as to show them to the terrace."

"Yes, Lady Hermione." Dingleby retreated, his face calm and composed, as if the "unfortunate accident" were of no interest whatsoever to him. I guess they have a course in that at butler school.

Within moments, the local bobby had arrived, as Dingleby informed his mistress when he came back bearing fresh tea. Not long after that, Robin and his crew appeared. Robin paused briefly to be introduced to Lady Hermione and Nina, explaining who he was and what he and his squad would be doing.

"Do you have a room we might use for interviewing witnesses?" Robin asked politely.

Lady Hermione waved a hand. "Just ask Dingleby. He will see to whatever you need."

"Thank you, Lady Hermione." Robin turned suavely to me. "Dr. Kirby-Jones, if I might have a word with you?" He nodded at Nina. "Miss Yaknova, I'd like to interview you next, but that won't be for a few minutes. If you would be so kind as to wait here for me."

"Certainly, Detective Inspector," Nina said in her sweetest tones. I could already see the wheels turning. Robin is a very attractive man, and Nina no doubt thought she would be able to charm him without much effort. Nina might just be surprised.

Out in the hallway, Robin turned to me, his expression stern. "What now, Simon? One begins to think you're like that American woman on the telly. What's her name, Fletcher? Everywhere she goes, a dead body turns up."

"Really, Robin," I protested. "I go lots of places where no one dies."

Robin's lips pursed. He really is most attractive, but he's also hard to read. I can never tell if he's flirting with me or if he simply finds me amusing. No doubt you can imagine which I'd prefer.

"Who is the victim, Simon? Tell me again."

"She claimed to be Dorinda Darlington, author of a highly successful series of detective novels featuring a female sleuth."

Robin picked up my slight emphasis on "claimed." "What do you mean? Was that not who she was?" Bright man; he follows verbal cues very quickly.

"No, she's not Dorinda Darlington. I'm not sure who she really was. I've been trying to find out, because I want to know why she was impersonating m—" I caught myself. "Impersonating Dorinda Darlington. I know the real Dorinda, and this woman is not she."

Robin's eyes narrowed at my stumble. "Then just who is the real Dorinda Darlington? That might have some bearing on this case."

Should I come clean with Robin? I had been secretive about Dorinda's real identity because the reading public might not be too happy to know that "her" books were written by a man. Leaving aside the fact, naturally, that the author was both gay and dead. The PC police might have a field day, and I wanted to stay *out* of the spotlight—natural behavior for a vampire.

But perhaps Robin could keep the secret and keep it from becoming "official" knowledge. "If I confide something in you, Robin, can you try to keep it under the table, as it were?"

Robin's right eyebrow rose interrogatively. "Perhaps, Simon, but you know I can't really promise that. If it has direct bearing upon what happened, I might not be able to hold it back."

That was just what I had expected him to say. Oh, well, in for a penny and all that.

"I am Dorinda Darlington. That's how I know she was an impostor."

His jaw dropped.

Then he recovered, and I watched him, almost seeing the wheels turn as he assessed this new piece of information. Had I just put myself at the head of the list of suspects?

Chapter Twelve

———— 💀 ————

Upon quick reflection, I decided I couldn't be too worried about being a serious suspect in the fake Dorinda's murder. After all, I had been in sight of someone ever since Dorinda had left the gathering earlier, on her way to meet her killer.

"Right," Robin said. "I'll talk with you further, Simon, but for now I must see what's going on outside."

I nodded as he turned on his heel and left me. Time enough later to give him my alibi.

Now I had to face Nina and Lady Hermione again. I was rather keen to get Nina alone at some point and grill her. I was convinced she knew far more than she was letting on about what the murder victim had been up to here at Kinsale House. If, indeed, Nina hadn't been behind the whole thing in the first place. But surely even Nina hadn't planned on murder.

Lady Hermione seemed to have recovered much of her accustomed sangfroid when I rejoined her and Nina in the drawing room. "Really, Nina," she was saying in her severest tones, "I cannot think why you should have subjected us all . . ." She ceased talking abruptly when she realized that I was once again in the room. "Well, Dr. Kirby-Jones? What has your friend the policeman to say about this dreadful situation?"

From her tone one would have thought poor Robin had come to empty the rubbish bins at Kinsale House. Nina cast an amused glance at our hostess, then rolled her eyes in my direction. "Yes, Simon, do tell us what that absolutely delicious copper had to say. Are you the prime suspect?" Her eyebrows arched in mockery.

All at once I was struck by the nasty suspicion that Nina had murdered the faux Dorinda—indeed, that she had stage-managed the entire fiasco—in order to manufacture some lurid story. I could see the headlines now, something totally trashy about a gay man murdering a woman to safeguard his identity as a female mystery writer. Such publicity would no doubt sell books, but I cringed at the thought.

I considered Nina's reaction upon finding the body. Nina was cold and calculating, but I didn't think she was that good an actress. Her surprise— and indeed, horror—at finding Dorinda's body had seemed very real, but if this were all part of her plan, perhaps she had fooled me into thinking her shock was real.

I quelled such useless speculation for the moment and directed at Nina my most repressive frown. "Don't be absurd, Nina! You know very well that, from the time Dorinda—or whoever she really was— left this room, I was in sight of someone, until I

found *you* on the terrace, not far from her corpse."
I grinned evilly. "For all I know, Nina, darling, you
pushed that urn on top of her head before I joined
you on the terrace."

"Now who's being absurd, Simon? I haven't the
strength to hurl that urn on top of Dorinda, or anyone else, for that matter!"

Lady Hermione examined the two of us with
disgust. "You are both utterly lacking in the remotest
sense of propriety!" She sniffed loudly. "But I must
say, Nina, that you are doing it up a bit too brown
if you want to convince us you're too frail to have
moved that urn. They weigh perhaps forty pounds—
or more, if you consider the soil and the plants
they contain. I've no doubt that you could find the
strength to shift something like that off the balustrade and onto that unfortunate woman's head!"

"Careful, Hermione," Nina said, her voice taut
with anger.

Lady Hermione flushed and said not another
word.

I wondered what hold Nina had over our hostess. Could it be that the late and unlamented (at
least on my part) faux Dorinda hadn't been the
only one with a taste for blackmail?

And, I reasoned further, if Nina and Dorinda
had been in cahoots, and if that relationship had
somehow soured, Nina could have killed Dorinda.

I rather liked that notion, I found, having totally
gone off Nina. I couldn't wait to find myself a new
agent here in the U.K.

Before I could think of some new conversational
gambit, Robin Chase returned to collect Nina for
an interview. I wished I could be a little bat on the
wall and listen to that session. I could imagine it all:
Nina would try her darnedest to flirt with Robin,

who in turn would be at his phlegmatic best in turning away such attempts on her part. How deliciously droll it would be, despite the gravity of the situation.

Left alone with my hostess, who was eyeing me uneasily, I decided I had better do something to redeem myself with her. While Lady Hermione fiddled with things on the tea tray, now studiously ignoring me, I sat down on the sofa nearest her chair.

"My dear Lady Hermione," I said, my voice like warm honey, "I can't tell you how much I regret that you should have to suffer these truly horrible disruptions to your program for the week. Everyone will be at sixes and sevens now. What can my assistant and I do to help you and Miss Monkley?"

"Very civil of you, Dr. Kirby-Jones," she said gruffly. "Nothing like this has ever occurred at Kinsale House, and certainly not during one of my writers' weeks. But that is by the by, now. Can't refine too much upon that! We'll have to do what we can to minimize the upset. Once the police have the mess tidied up, we can go about our business."

"Yes, of course, Lady Hermione," I replied. "But it might take a while for the police to figure out who the murderer is. In the meantime, I'm not sure there's much we can do. The police might wish to send everyone home, after they've all been interviewed, of course."

"Nonsense!" Lady Hermione barked. "The police can investigate, and we shall go on with our program."

"I suppose that's possible," I said, though privately I wasn't certain just what Robin would think of such a plan. He might be happy, however, to keep all his suspects in one place for a few days.

Lady Hermione looked up as the door opened

and Isabella Veryan entered, in considerable agitation.

"Hermione! What is this I hear about that wretched woman being found dead—no, murdered!—out on the terrace?" Isabella collapsed on the sofa next to me, and I turned to her with sympathy. Her skin had lost all its color, and her lips trembled.

"Afraid it's true, Belle," Lady Hermione said, her voice oddly gentle. She and Isabella stared at each other, engaged in some sort of silent communication. I could read desperation and fear in Isabella, stoic calm in Lady Hermione, neither of which emotions was of much help in figuring out what they were trying to keep hidden from me.

"What can this mean?" Isabella cried. "Who among us would do such a thing? And why?" This melodramatic turn on Isabella's part made me curious. She hadn't seemed the type to indulge in histrionics of this nature.

"I haven't the least notion, Belle," Lady Hermione responded, her tone becoming brisker. "Buck up, girl; don't let this overset you! We shall weather the storm; never fear."

Isabella almost literally stank of fear. I recalled the cryptic threat with which Dorinda had taunted her, and I wondered what skeleton in her closet Isabella didn't want revealed. Surely it couldn't be anything that terrible. But she was of a more intensely private generation, after all, and while I might think her peccadilloes not all that titillating, she could very well see them in a different light. Ostensibly, Nina wasn't the only one with a motive to want Dorinda out of the way, but would Isabella have killed to safeguard her secret?

Before I could think of a way to ask a question, the door once again opened, and Giles strode in.

"I beg your pardon, Lady Hermione, but I must speak urgently with Dr. Kirby-Jones." He stood, waiting.

"Certainly, young man." Lady Hermione positively beamed at Giles for his show of good manners.

I got up from the sofa and approached Giles. He led me a few steps away from Lady Hermione and Isabella, who fell into a low-voiced conversation the moment they thought we were out of earshot. I wanted to listen to them, but Giles's manner was too urgent.

"Yes, what is it, Giles? Have you found out something?"

We had paused near the door, and Giles opened his mouth, about to speak, when the door opened. Norah Tattersall strode in, literally dragging the local constable by the arm.

She came to a halt just inside the door and pointed at Giles with a flourish worthy of Sarah Bernhardt.

"There he is, Officer! Arrest him immediately!"

At first I couldn't discern whether she was pointing at me or at Giles, but from the way Giles suddenly turned pale, I knew he was the target of Norah's accusation.

"What on earth are you gabbling about, Miss Tattersall?" I asked, striving to keep my tone mild. "Are you accusing my assistant of something?"

Norah's mouth widened in a triumphant grin. "I saw him on the terrace not an hour ago, arguing with that poor woman. He killed her!"

Chapter Thirteen

Giles tensed beside me, and I laid a reassuring hand on his arm. He might be impetuous, but he is not a killer. He very well might have been arguing with the late unlamented on the terrace, but he hadn't killed her. I would have been able to read his guilt—he's still not terribly sophisticated at hiding his deepest emotions, particularly from me.

"Nonsense!" I said, my voice at its deepest and most authoritative.

Norah Tattersall blinked and took a step backward. "But I saw him!" Her tone was much less firm.

"You might have seen him talking to her," I said, "but you did not see him attack her or harm her, did you?"

"Well, no," she said with great reluctance. She made an effort to reassert herself. "But he was very angry with her!"

By now Giles had calmed down. "Yes, I'll admit I

was arguing with her," he said in his best young-lord-of-the-manor manner. "But I never touched her. When I left her on the terrace, she was still alive. Someone came along after that and harmed her. It wasn't I who killed her, I can assure you!"

"Of course not," I said, eyeing Norah Tattersall with great disfavor. She wilted under such strong opposition to her absurd claims.

"Moreover," Giles said loftily, "I shall be quite happy to inform Detective Inspector Chase of the subject of my conversation with the so-called Dorinda Darlington." He turned to me. "I found out who she really is, Simon."

Both Norah and the young constable perked up at this. "Oh, really?" Norah asked, moving closer.

"What's that, Mr. Blitherington?" Lady Hermione called from where she had been conversing with Isabella Veryan. "What have you learned?"

"I beg your pardon, Lady Hermione," Giles said smoothly, "but I fear I must disappoint you for the moment. I believe I should wait and tell the detective inspector what I've learned, and then he may inform everyone as he sees fit."

"Fustian!" I muttered, and Giles shot me a sideways grin. He would tell *me* what he had found out, even if he was reluctant to share it with the rest of the room.

"Very well." Lady Hermione frowned, but she made no attempt to dissuade Giles from his intention to keep mum.

"Trust you, Norah, to make an ass of yourself," Isabella Veryan observed acidly.

Norah Tattersall flushed a most unbecoming shade of red. Without another word, she turned and fled the room. The young constable she had dragged into the room stared at the floor, uncertain what to do. Should he follow her, in ignominious defeat, or stay and listen?

"If you would be so good, Officer," I addressed him, and he perked up, "please let the detective inspector know, as soon as you can, that we have some important information for him."

He nodded, relieved at having something to do. He ducked his head in the direction of Lady Hermione and Isabella, then left us.

Before Isabella or Lady Hermione made an attempt to question Giles or me further, I, too, nodded in their direction. "If you'll excuse us, dear ladies, Giles and I will now seek out the detective inspector."

Lady Hermione inclined her head. "Certainly, Dr. Kirby-Jones."

Once the door was closed safely behind us, I drew Giles into an alcove in the hall and demanded that he tell me what had happened before we went to talk to Robin Chase.

Giles grinned. "I decided, Simon, to take the most expedient route to finding out just who she was."

"And what expedient route was that, Giles?"

"I let myself into her room when I knew she was elsewhere, and I had a recce through her things."

"Certainly expedient, if less than ethical. If I weren't so interested in what you found, I'd reprimand you," I observed wryly. "And pray tell, what did you discover?"

"She had made no attempt to hide her true identity. With very little effort I found her driving license and several other papers." Giles paused, drawing out the revelations.

"Yes?" I said impatiently. "Who was she?"

"Her name was Wanda Harper," Giles responded,

still grinning. "And according to what I found in her purse, she had quite a healthy balance in her building society account."

"Blackmail payments," I suggested.

"Perhaps," Giles said. "Or it could simply be her salary from her job."

"Which was?" I feared my tone was getting quite testy by this point.

"She was an employee of the Yaknova Literary Agency." Giles reached into a pocket and withdrew a card, which he handed to me.

There, in black-and-white print, was the truth. Wanda Harper had been, according to the card, an associate of Nina's.

I muttered a few words that were less than complimentary to Nina's forebears.

"Precisely," Giles said with great satisfaction. "The bloody cow must have set this whole thing up deliberately."

"But why?" I could think of several reasons, all of which reinforced my desire to sever my business relationship with Ms. Yaknova.

Giles shrugged. "Perhaps your favorite copper can get her to confess."

Giles is not overly fond of Robin Chase, since he suspects—quite rightly—that I find the detective inspector an attractive enigma. An enigma, I might add, that I would enjoy investigating further, given the chance. Alas, however, Robin has thus far firmly resisted my attempts to delve into his dating preferences.

Someone coughed nearby. I had been so intent on what Giles and I had been discussing that I had not heard anyone approach us. The local bobby stood waiting.

"Yes, Officer?" I asked.

"Detective Inspector Chase will see you now, sir," he said, stepping back and indicating that I should follow him.

"Thank you, Officer," I said as Giles and I came along obediently behind him.

Dingleby, the butler, had set up Robin and his sergeant, whose name I couldn't recall for the moment, in the library of Kinsale House. A spacious chamber with high ceilings, it must have contained some twenty or thirty thousand volumes. It was also one of the few rooms I had thus far seen in this monstrous pile that didn't make me shudder at the appalling taste of the Kinsale family. This room, unlike any other chamber I had seen, was actually attractive and looked like what one expected the library of an aristocratic family should.

Robin sat behind a huge mahogany desk, scribbling away in a notebook, but he put his pen aside and rose as Giles and I approached him. Robin nodded a greeting at Giles. "I believe, Sir Giles"—Robin always insisted on using Giles's title, which courtesy Giles detested—"that you have information you wish to impart?"

"Yes, Detective Inspector Chase," Giles said, his tony accent become slightly more upper class and nasal, "I do. I have discovered the true identity of the murder victim."

Robin waved a hand at us, indicating that we should have a seat.

"Yes, I believe her real name"—Robin made a pretense of consulting his notebook as he seated himself—"was Wanda Harper. She lived in Chelsea."

Giles was not completely deflated at having his bit of thunder stolen. "You found her purse, I see."

Robin vouchsafed a small smile. "Naturally, Sir Giles. That's the first thing my men looked for, after we had secured the crime scene."

I had had enough of this little pissing contest—if you'll pardon the vulgarity. "Did you also see, Robin," I said impatiently, "that Miss Wanda Harper was an employee of Nina Yaknova's literary agency?"

Robin regarded me with a bland gaze. "Yes, Simon, we had noted that as well. In fact, I talked with Miss Yaknova about that in my interview with her. She confirmed that Miss Harper was indeed an employee of hers."

Nina had apparently done an abrupt about-face. "Did Nina happen to explain to you, perchance, why Miss Harper had embarked on this impersonation of Dorinda Darlington? And why she was playing along with it?"

Robin glanced down at his notes. "According to Miss Yaknova, Simon, this charade was all part of a publicity campaign for the forthcoming new novel by Dorinda Darlington." He paused for a moment, to let that sink in. "Moreover, Miss Yaknova claims that you, the real 'Dorinda Darlington,' had agreed to the plan."

"Preposterous! I did no such thing," I contested hotly. "Whatever little scheme Nina had cooked up with this Wanda Harper person, she did so without any encouragement or approval from me."

"Bloody cow!" Giles muttered, just loud enough for Robin to hear.

Robin ignored him. "Also according to Miss Yaknova, you, Simon, were unaccountably failing to play your role in the scheme. Instead, Miss Yaknova claims, you suddenly became confrontational, which was not what Miss Yaknova had wanted."

Nina was more slippery than the proverbial eel. What a farrago of nonsense she had fed Robin! I still hadn't figured out completely what her objective in all this had been, but at the moment, most likely, she was doing her best to divert suspicion away from herself and toward me or Giles.

"Nina's full of it," I said bluntly.

Robin quirked an eyebrow at me interrogatively.

"I never agreed to any such plan," I reiterated. "Whatever little scheme Nina had dreamed up, she was executing it without any prior knowledge or approval on my part."

"Simon knew nothing about any of this," Giles asserted, his voice rising in anger.

"As far as you're aware, Sir Giles," Robin qualified.

Giles was about ready to launch himself across the desk at Robin's throat, but I laid a restraining hand on his arm. "Temper, temper," I said softly. Giles subsided in his chair, but I could feel him still boiling mad beside me.

"Nina is playing some deep game of her own, Robin," I said in as quiet and authoritative a manner as I could. "Perhaps when you discover just what that game is, you might be closer to knowing who killed Wanda Harper. I didn't do it, and neither did Giles."

"We do have a witness who places Sir Giles on the terrace not too long before the victim was killed." Robin addressed me, but he was watching Giles very carefully while not appearing to do so.

With great effort Giles had mastered his temper. "Yes, Detective Inspector Chase, I freely admit that I talked with Miss Harper on the terrace. We did indeed argue, and if anyone were listening, he or she would have heard raised voices. I confronted her with her true identity, and she responded angrily."

"Did she attempt to strike you, Sir Giles?" Robin queried smoothly.

"No," Giles said. "Why would she do that?"

"Perhaps she struck out at you, and in attempting to defend yourself, you struck back?"

I hadn't seen this side of Robin before. While it was most definitely professional, it was not attractive. I didn't like to see Giles treated this way, but I knew I had to let him answer for himself.

Being able to trace one's aristocratic lineage back nearly to the Conquest does pay off sometimes, and this was one of those occasions. With all the dignity of generations of noble Blitheringtons behind him, Giles said, "I have never in my life struck a woman, Detective Inspector. I did use harsh language with her because I found her deceit appalling, but I did not accost her physically."

I could read the reluctant admiration in Robin's eyes. Almost against his will, I think, he believed Giles. "Very well, Sir Giles," he said. "We will continue interviewing witnesses, and perhaps we will find someone who saw Miss Harper alive after you left the terrace." He stood up. "Until then, gentlemen, if you will be so kind as to refrain from sharing any of what we have discussed with anyone else here at Kinsale House."

With that, we were dismissed.

Chapter Fourteen

———— ☠ ————

Lady Hermione's program for the remainder of the day had to be scrapped, though Lady Hermione herself would, I think, have been perfectly happy to continue as if nothing untoward had occurred. One would prefer not to acknowledge the fact of a murder on the premises of one's stately home, of course, but the rather pesky presence of the authorities meant that Lady Hermione had perforce to follow Robin Chase's wishes in the matter. We thus spent much of the afternoon twiddling our thumbs idly in our rooms while we waited for the police to finish interviewing everyone in the house.

I spent quite some time in speculating upon just what Nina's role in this brouhaha was. Had she engineered the whole scenario for some devious purpose of her own? Or had it started that way, and someone else had come along and hijacked her plot, so to speak?

Giles was spending the time more profitably. He had brought along his laptop computer and was busy roaming through cyberspace, finding out what he could about some of our fellow guests. I had expressed my doubts that he might find something truly useful among all the wealth of disinformation out there, but he merely smiled and told me to wait and see. I went back to my endless ruminations.

By the time the summons came for tea, Giles had amassed a stack of papers for his labors. "Anything useful?" I asked.

"I trust you will find it so eventually, Simon," he said, shutting down his computer. Standing and stretching, he smiled at me again. "All of your fellow authors have various Web sites devoted to them, and I've found a number of interviews here and there on the Web for each of them. Not too many surprises, but I did find a few inconsistencies here and there. They might come to nothing, but I'll do a bit more checking. We shall see."

He refused to give me any other hints, so I decided not to force the issue. He had appointed himself Watson to my Holmes; so be it.

Downstairs, we found the group assembled for tea rather sparse in number. "I suppose many of them elected to have tea in their rooms or to skip it altogether," Giles said in a low voice as we surveyed the room.

"Perhaps they feared someone would poison the tea," I suggested half-seriously.

"Very likely." Giles snorted. "No doubt they think there's a mass murderer on the loose, just looking for his or her next victim."

"I could suggest at least one candidate for that position." I scowled in Nina's direction, and she affected not to notice me, being heavily involved in a conversation with Ashford Dunn.

"I doubt we need to imagine what those two have spent the afternoon doing," Giles said, snickering.

"Tut, tut, Giles," I said, "keep your **mind out of the gutter.**"

He laughed heartily at that, and **I couldn't resist** joining him. Almost as if he knew our laughter was directed at him, Dunn stared hard at us, then pointedly turned his back to us.

"Simon!" Isabella Veryan called to me, and Giles and I sauntered over to join her. She patted the sofa next to her, and I sank down beside her. Giles moved off toward the tea tray after I indicated that I cared for nothing.

"How are you, Isabella? How was your session with Detective Inspector Chase?"

"What a charming and perspicacious young man!" Isabella practically purred with satisfaction. "He appeared far more interested in discussing my work than in asking me questions about the unfortunate events here. He complimented me, and quite handsomely, on the accuracy of my depiction of police methods in my books."

Knowing Robin as I did, I had no doubt he was sincere in his appreciation of Isabella Veryan's literary efforts, but I also figured he had, without Isabella's realizing he was doing so, questioned her adeptly about her movements. She was a shrewd old girl, but Robin had charmed her so effectively she probably hadn't noticed what he was really after.

"Yes, he's very charming and very, very intelligent," I acknowledged. "He will soon sort out this whole mess, I'm sure."

"I doubt he'll have to look very far," Isabella said. Her eyes narrowed as she stared at someone across the room. I followed her gaze, and she had fixed upon Nina and young Dunn.

"You think Nina is responsible?"

Isabella suddenly became fascinated by the pleats in her sensible tweed skirt. "Nina can be a remarkably effective agent, don't you think, Simon?"

"Yes," I said, "but before the last day or so, I had no idea what some of her methods were."

"Nina is not always ethical."

"Apparently not. Though I'm just now coming to realize that, Isabella. Perhaps you were more aware of that than I, before now?"

At last she gave over playing with her skirt and looked me in the eyes. "For a long time, Simon, I simply closed my eyes and let Nina have her way. After all, my books were selling well. Selling better and better with each new book, and Nina had a lot to do with that. She was most aggressive in dealing with my longtime publishers and getting them to market my books much more effectively. I had no complaints on that score, though I sometimes found Nina's notions of appropriate publicity a bit . . . odd, shall we say?"

"I have not sought out the spotlight, and I know Nina has chafed at that," I said. "But in the last year or two, you've been much in the public eye, haven't you?"

Isabella nodded.

"No doubt you have found that exhausting," I said when she made no further comment. "All those public appearances must take a toll on one's energy, not to mention the fact that it eats away at one's writing time." I forbore to add the words *particularly for someone of your age.*

"Exactly!" The word burst from Isabella's lips. "I tried, again and again, to explain to Nina how wearing I found all these dog-and-pony shows she insisted that I do, and she kept insisting that they were necessary if I wanted to keep selling books like I had begun to do. If I wanted a better advance for the next book, and so on, then I would have to agree to do what the publisher wanted, and keep my name before the reading public. Not only here in England, but in the United States and on the Continent as well."

"Would your sales really suffer that much if you simply put your foot down and stayed home?"

Isabella sighed heavily. "I would like to think not, but how can one judge that? For many years I made a respectable, if not luxurious, living with my work. Then, about five years ago, my sales suddenly took off, and I made the best-seller lists for the first time. Ever since then, there has been increased pressure to sell more and more."

I was struck by a sudden idea. "When did Nina become your agent?"

Isabella looked away. "About seven years ago."

"And before that time," I hazarded a guess, "you rarely made public appearances, didn't attend mystery conventions, talk much to the press, and so on."

She shook her head. "I lived the way I preferred: quietly. I was able to devote myself to my writing."

"But that wasn't enough for Nina."

"No, she told me from the beginning, when I first signed with her, that she thought I wasn't selling up to my potential, and that she could make me wealthy."

"And so you signed with her?" I regarded her quizzically. Something about all this wasn't quite adding up.

Isabella shifted uncomfortably, once again avoiding looking at me. "I did."

"Something about what she was offering must have appealed to you, then."

Isabella had begun to look as if she deeply regretted calling me over for this little tête-à-tête. "I suppose all writers must long for more recognition, bigger sales, and all that."

I couldn't argue with that. I didn't write simply for my own amusement, nor did Isabella. All writers want an audience, the bigger the better. Any writer who tells you he doesn't want to be a bestseller is lying.

Isabella, however, was lying about something. I couldn't quite put my finger on it, but something had made her quite uncomfortable. Otherwise she wouldn't have attempted to evade me with such a cliché.

"I simply detest being in the spotlight," Isabella said unexpectedly. "Unlike some."

I followed her gaze, and she was once again regarding Nina and Dunn with loathing.

"Yes, our Mr. Dunn seems quite happy as the focus of attention."

"Perhaps he believes his handsome face and toothsome smile make up for the fact that he can't write." The venom in Isabella's voice surprised me. "I'll admit that I did try to read one of his books, but I found it not to my taste."

"Nina had the nerve to ask me to write a blurb for him!" Isabella was nearly bouncing on the sofa, she was so agitated. "I read as much of his swill as I could force myself to, but it makes John Grisham look like a Nobel laureate."

I laughed. "That doesn't mean it won't sell, and sell big."

Isabella shuddered. "Unfortunately not. I had the truly delightful experience of seeing my name and his on the same best-seller list. For his second book, and my twentieth!"

"Whatever her faults, Nina does have an eye for what will sell."

"I'm not gainsaying that, Simon," Isabella muttered. "But I despise having to be associated with that talentless hack!"

"Going off about young Dunn again, eh, Isabella?"

George Austen-Hare clumped to a stop in front of the sofa we occupied. Despite the fact that he was standing and I was seated, our eyes were almost on a level. I had to tilt my head only slightly to look up into his face. He was grinning.

"Told you, old girl, to ignore the blighter. Twenty years from now, whom do you think they'll still be reading?" He slurped noisily at his tea. "You and me, m'dear, not that young wanker. No matter how pretty he is."

"If I'm still around in twenty years, George, dear, and not totally gaga, perhaps I'll take comfort in that fact." Isabella had collected herself enough to smile at Austen-Hare.

"You'll see old bones yet, Isabella." Austen-Hare smiled back seraphically.

"Dear George," Isabella said. "Thank heavens for good friends like you."

He harrumphed into his tea, embarrassed by Isabella's fond tone. "Pity that urn fell on the wrong head."

"What do you mean?" I asked.

Austen-Hare nodded in Nina's direction. "Should have been that witch. Dunno how she's escaped being murdered this long."

"George! You really shouldn't say such things!" I

couldn't quite buy the tone of outrage in Isabella's voice. I already knew she hated and feared Nina, but I was curious why Austen-Hare also loathed her.

Before I could question either of them further, squeals of outrage erupted across the room. Startled, we turned as one to look.

Patty Anne Putney had knocked Nina to the floor and was busily pounding her head against the carpet, while Mr. Murbles lay nearby, his head neatly separated from the rest of his small body.

Chapter Fifteen

Everyone in the room had frozen in place, watching the fight. Nina attempted to retaliate by gouging at Patty Anne's eyes, but Patty Anne kept dodging Nina's hands, all the while pounding Nina's head up and down. Then the room surged into motion as Giles and the butler, Dingleby, ran forward to separate the two women. Everyone else, myself included, got up from our seats and converged around the battle scene.

Giles had grabbed Nina, pulling her up off the floor, and Dingleby held Patty Anne. Both women were struggling to break free to go at it again, but Giles and the butler were taller and much stronger than either of them, and they held fast to their separate combatants.

"Nina! Patricia Anne!" Lady Hermione's voice cut through the babble, and suddenly quiet reigned. I took an involuntary step backward.

"What is the meaning of this outrageous behavior?" Lady Hermione now stood between the two women, and at her signal, Giles and Dingleby released them.

"Why have you subjected us all to such a vulgar display?" Lady Hermione addressed this question to Nina, but Patty Anne Putney answered.

"Murderer! That's what you are! Look at what you've done!" She pointed at the floor, where poor, decapitated Mr. Murbles lay, his head several inches from his plush little body. A bit of stuffing extruded from the neck.

"Nina, how could you do such a vicious thing?" Lady Hermione said, her voice thick with disgust, as Dexter Harbaugh came forward to clasp a sobbing Patty Anne in his arms. He stroked her hair and murmured in her ear in an attempt to comfort her.

Nina massaged the back of her head with one hand. "I'm going to bring charges against that lunatic," she said, her voice low and angry. Ashford Dunn was attempting to comfort her, but she waved him away. He retreated a few paces and pouted.

"Answer my question, Nina!" Lady Hermione took a step closer to Nina.

"Honestly, Hermione," she said. "I simply did what all of us have been longing to do. I was tired of pretending to talk to that absurd stuffed animal of hers, and I snapped. Before I knew it, the thing was in my hands and I had ripped its head off. Then *she* went berserk and attacked me!"

"How could you do such a thing to her, you cow?" Dexter Harbaugh made as if to approach Nina, but Lady Hermione held up a hand. I recalled having heard Harbaugh himself threaten Mr. Murbles yesterday, but now that he was playing the role of sensitive and supportive man, I supposed he had forgotten that little lapse.

"Watch out for that spider, Dexter!" Nina said, raising her voice a bit and pointing somewhere behind Harbaugh.

Startled, Harbaugh released Patty Anne Putney and whirled around. "Where?" His voice had risen at least an octave.

"My mistake." Nina grinned evilly as Harbaugh turned back to face her, a murderous glint in his eyes.

"You bloody cow," he said.

"Isn't it nice, Nina," I said, "to have all the members of your little fan club all together like this?"

Giles quickly smothered a laugh, while the eyes of the company turned to me. I smiled.

Lady Hermione ignored me. "Nina, I'm appalled at your behavior. You will leave this house at once!"

"I'm afraid, Lady Hermione," said Robin Chase, "that I must overrule you in that request."

Unnoticed by the rest of us, Dingleby had slipped away to summon the police.

"Must she really stay here, Detective Inspector?" Lady Hermione had steel in her voice.

Robin was a match for her. "It would be much more convenient, ma'am."

"As you wish." Lady Hermione turned back to Nina. "But as soon as the detective inspector allows it, Nina, I want you to leave."

"Don't worry, Hermione, dear," Nina cooed, "I won't stay a minute longer than I'm forced to." She smoothed down her dress. "Detective Inspector, I'd like to speak with you about pressing charges for assault."

"Certainly, Miss Yaknova," Robin said. "I'll speak with you now, and then with Miss Putney, if I may."

He inclined his head toward Patty Anne. She sniffed and nodded, her sobs having ceased.

Robin led Nina from the room as the rest of us watched in silence. Glowering at us all, Ashford Dunn followed them from the room, like a little boy who knows he's no longer welcome at the party.

Dexter Harbaugh had picked up Mr. Murbles from the floor and was cuddling the stuffed bunny, its head jammed back in place, in his arms. Patty Anne smiled tremulous thanks for his solicitude.

"If you'll permit me, Dexter," Lady Hermione said, "one of the maids is quite adept at, er, repairs of this nature." She held out her hands, and Harbaugh gratefully dumped both pieces of Mr. Murbles into them. "My dear, don't worry, he'll be good as new, and very soon." She waited a moment for Patty Anne's nod of permission, then sailed from the room, bearing her wounded charge. The few remaining conference attendees trailed after her, leaving just six of us in the room.

Isabella Veryan approached Patty Anne and placed a consoling arm around her shoulders. She drew her toward a sofa while instructing Dexter Harbaugh quietly to fetch a cup of hot, sweet tea.

"My dear, I know this was a terrible shock to you," Isabella said, making Patty Anne comfortable beside her. "But what on earth precipitated such an act? I know Nina is very temperamental, but I've never seen her behave like this."

Patty Anne's tearstained face took on a mutinous look. "I'd really prefer not to discuss it, Isabella, if you wouldn't mind."

Isabella patted her hand, then released it as Harbaugh approached with the tea. She waited while Patty Anne had a moment to sip at the tea; then she persisted gently. "I know it's distressing for you, my dear, but surely you can understand why we're all so concerned."

Patty Anne appealed to Dexter Harbaugh with her eyes, and he nodded.

"Very well, then," Patty Anne said. "If you must know, Nina was bullying me. She wanted me to sign with her again, after I had fired her a few months ago. I told her there was no way I would ever work with her again. Mr. Murbles . . ." and here she threatened to break down again. She took a deep breath and gained control of herself before continuing. "Mr. Murbles and I both despise her and her shabby methods. I told her so, in no uncertain terms, and that's when . . . that's when . . ." Her lip trembled, and she could speak no further.

"We quite understand, my dear," Isabella said soothingly. She looked at George Austen-Hare for a moment, then sought out Dexter Harbaugh. "We all know Nina only too well. You need explain no further."

I wanted to stamp my foot in frustration. The four of them were privy to something about Nina that I didn't know. They had all been clients of hers longer than I, and they had all been bigger sellers than I, at least until very recently. What had Nina done to them to deserve such rancor on their part?

Perhaps more important, what had Nina been planning to do to me?

If I knew the answer to that, I reasoned, I might be closer to knowing who had murdered Wanda Harper, and why. Somehow, I figured, the two must be connected.

"Woman ought to be struck off, or some such," Harbaugh commented, watching Patty Anne through narrowed eyes. She offered yet another tremulous smile to his gruff words. I had begun to see her appeal to a man like Dexter Harbaugh, who despised her weakness at the same time he craved it.

"Yes, after what I've seen this weekend, it's truly amazing to me that Nina keeps any clients whatsoever," I said, glancing from face to face to gauge the effects of my words. "I certainly won't have anything more to do with her after this weekend. She's fired, and that's that. I can't imagine that any of you would continue to retain her after the way she's behaved here this weekend."

Isabella shifted uncomfortably on the sofa beside Patty Anne. She did not meet my eyes as she responded to my challenge. "Simon, dear boy, I'm afraid that ending a business relationship with Nina is not so simple as you might imagine."

"Yes, I know that she'll retain rights to income on certain titles, ones for which she negotiated contracts and so on, but that doesn't mean one is tied to her forever."

George Austen-Hare, who had been unaccountably silent for some time, started sputtering and coughing. We all turned to him to see what was the matter. His face had turned an alarming shade of red, and at first I thought he had swallowed something the wrong way and might be choking.

Then I realized he was laughing.

"What's so funny?" I asked.

It took him a moment, but George mastered himself long enough to sputter, "The only way to get rid of Nina is to kill her." Then he dissolved into laughter once more, sounding more and more hysterical. Dexter Harbaugh approached him and thumped him hard on the back several times, and George finally subsided.

After that, one could have heard the proverbial pin drop in the room.

Isabella Veryan gazed knowingly at Dexter Harbaugh, who regarded her without blinking. Then one eyebrow arched slightly, and Isabella nodded once, decisively, in return.

"Simon, dear, if you wouldn't mind, we'd like to talk to you." Isabella glanced meaningfully in Giles's direction.

I took the hint. "Giles, if you wouldn't mind, could you go and continue that research we were talking about earlier?" I wouldn't have minded having Giles hear whatever they were about to tell me, but if it made them more comfortable to talk to me alone, then I'd play along.

Giles frowned, disappointed at being sent away from the fun, but he acceded to my request with good grace. He knew full well I'd tell him all about it later on anyway.

The moment the door closed behind Giles, Isabella said briskly, "What we're about to confide, Simon, must not leave this room. Do I have your promise?"

Examining each of their anxious faces in turn, I felt suddenly as if I had stumbled into an Enid Blyton adventure, where all the boys and girls had to swear solemn oaths and all that. Suppressing a grin, I replied, "Certainly, Isabella. I know how to respect confidences."

"Very well, then," Isabella said. "I feel it only fair to tell you, and I presume the rest of you are agreeable?" She paused for a moment, listening to the murmurs of assent from Patty Anne, Dexter, and George, before continuing. "None of us has dealt willingly with Nina in recent years, Simon. Though in many ways she is quite a good agent, she has other qualities that make working with her quite a trial."

Isabella paused again, and before she could resume dancing around the point, I said bluntly, "You mean because she's been blackmailing all of you?"

Chapter Sixteen

None of them made any sounds of denial. Instead they sat there staring at me, their faces blank. I didn't think I'd like to play poker with any of them, even Patty Anne, who hadn't, before now, impressed me as being particularly strong-minded about anything.

"Sorry, Isabella," I said, "to ruin your big moment of revelation, but it didn't take too long to figure out. You all obviously detest Nina, even fear her. I had to ask myself, if that were the case, why on earth you continued to be clients of hers when there are no doubt many agents who would jump at the chance to represent any one of you. Ergo, I figured you must have some reason why you felt you couldn't fire Nina."

"You're too sharp by half, Simon," Isabella said, her voice light and playful, belying the baleful look in her eyes.

I wasn't going to be so ill-bred as to ask her *what* Nina was blackmailing her, or any of them, over, because I knew they wouldn't tell me—at least not now, not here. When I said nothing further, Isabella relaxed and the others exhaled. I smiled encouragingly at them.

"As you no doubt see, Simon," Isabella said, retaining her role as spokesperson for the group, "this situation calls for a certain amount of delicacy."

"You mean because all of you could be considered suspects, should Nina turn up dead?"

I had said it in a jesting tone, but nevertheless they all flinched.

"Guess we could say the same thing of you," Dexter Harbaugh growled at me.

"A hit, a palpable hit," I acknowledged, essaying a small bow in his direction.

Harbaugh scowled while Isabella permitted a smile to flit across her face.

"I suppose I *might* have a reason to wish Nina out of the way," I said. "I'm sure we all have little secrets in our pasts that we wouldn't care to have our readers know about. Now, would we?"

They all stared at me, as if they were watching an exotic species of animal that they had never seen before. "I, for example, would rather not have the reading public know that 'Dorinda Darlington' is really Simon Kirby-Jones. Some people simply don't think men can write credible female protagonists in a mystery series. My sales might suffer if that were widely known. Besides which, I'd rather stay home and write the books than go out on publicity tours and all that."

No one took the bait. They continued to stare at me. I did my best to gauge their emotions, but at the moment, they all seemed reasonably calm and unafraid. If one of them was the killer, he or she was certainly playing it very cool.

"Not, I grant you, a terribly compelling motive for killing someone," I said.

"At least, not a compelling motive to kill Nina," Harbaugh observed, stressing the name ever so slightly.

George Austen-Hare nodded vigorously. "But a demmed good motive for killing that other woman, whosiwhatsis." He coughed. "After all, there she was, pretending to be you, stealing your thunder a bit."

Nice return of serve, I thought. *Interesting double-team approach.* "But, again, not a terribly compelling motive for murder, wouldn't you say?" I smiled in derision. "After all, I could easily prove the truth of the matter. And I certainly had nothing to gain from the publicity from being arrested for murder."

"Except, possibly, a gigantic boost in sales." Harbaugh smiled triumphantly at that. "The reading public being the salacious gits they are."

"Rather difficult to enjoy, however, if one were languishing behind bars, wouldn't you say?" I smiled back at him.

"Enough of this." Isabella stood up. "I thought, in all fairness to you, Simon, that you should be aware of some aspects of the situation. But that is all we can tell you, and I'm sure you can understand why. Be on your guard with Nina, Simon, and don't trust her an inch. And as soon as this is settled, get the hell out of Dodge." She arched an eyebrow interrogatively. "Isn't that the expression?"

"Well said, Isabella," I acknowledged. I wanted to delve further into their reasons for fearing Nina, but I knew that I'd have to approach each of them separately if I hoped to get anything out of them.

For a moment I longed for the days when a vampire could put the "glamour" on someone and coerce him or her to do the vampire's will. Alas, that was one of the handy little parlor tricks that had gone by the wayside with the pills I took. Such is the price of progress, I suppose. I'd just have to worm the dirty details out of them the old-fashioned way, with nothing but my natural charm.

Which is considerable, of course.

As I watched them file out of the room, I pondered my next move. The last one of them was barely out the door before Giles came striding in, right on cue. He does have a knack for turning up when I have need of him.

"Giles, how good of you to anticipate me," I said.

He grinned. "And what is your command, sire?"

"Insolent lackey!" I responded, giving in to the impulse to banter. His grin grew wider. "Enough of that! To the business at hand."

"Which would be . . . ?"

"For one thing, we have to dig even further into the connections between the late and very unlamented Wanda Harper and our own dear, vicious Nina. Not to mention the dirt that Nina seems to have on our celebrity authors."

Giles's eyebrows rose at that last remark. "Blackmail, eh?"

I do like a man who's quick off the mark. "Exactly, Giles. Nina is blackmailing my fellow writers. Keeping them in line, keeping them tied to her—by foul means, evidently. I'm going to see what I can do to ferret out the skeletons in the cupboard. If you'll forgive the mixing of metaphors."

"While I find out more about Wanda Harper, I take it?"

I laughed. "Don't sound so disappointed, Giles.

I'm sure there are various juicy bits and bobs to uncover relating to Ms. Harper. I won't have all the fun."

He pouted his lips at me. "Somehow I doubt that, Simon. I do all the grunt work, and you have all the fun. Dedicated workers need rewards, too, you know."

The leer he gave me left me in little doubt as to the kind of reward he'd prefer. "Be off with you," I said, repressing a smile. "Go tote some barges."

He clicked his heels together and bowed. *"Ja wohl, mein Führer."* He raised his arm in a familiar salute.

At least he spared me the sight of him goose-stepping out of the room.

I stood for a moment in the quiet of the room, pondering my next move. I was eager to approach one of my fellow writers to try to worm out something further about Nina's blackmail activities, but I figured I had better wait just a little while before I tried. Better to let them all stew a bit first.

I decided that I would have another look, if I could, at the scene of the crime. I hadn't had much time earlier to look around, and I might not be able to see much, even now, because I was sure that Robin's team had cordoned off much of the area. Despite this, however, I might see something of use.

A couple of minutes later I was cautiously easing open the door to the terrace and peering out. The sky was still dark with clouds, though the rain had stopped. I didn't need to worry about dark glasses, hat, and gloves. I stepped out onto the terrace, pulling the door shut behind me.

Ahead of me I could see the canopy that Robin's crew had erected over the spot where Wanda Harper had lain. There was a PC on guard near the steps leading down to the grounds, and I nodded in friendly fashion in his direction. He inclined his head to acknowledge my presence and thereafter kept a watchful eye on me, should I attempt to move too close.

There was no point in my trying to examine the ground around where the body had been found, because Robin's team would have found anything of value there. What I wanted was a look at Kinsale House itself, from the vantage point of the terrace. I strode a few paces down the terrace toward the vigilant PC and stopped. Turning my back upon the young man, I surveyed the facade of the house.

Kinsale House was such a vast pile of a place that I still hadn't been able to put together a mental map of it. Had I had the chance to explore it completely, I could have figured out what I wanted to know without having to come out on the terrace. I gazed up at the wing of the house above me, and I nodded in satisfaction.

Just as I had thought. This wing of the house, which looked out over the terrace, was the one in which my fellow writers and I were quartered. Even as I looked up at the windows, a curtain twitched, and I spotted George Austen-Hare staring down at me. The moment he realized I had seen him, he let the curtain fall and stepped back from the window.

The other conference attendees were housed in another wing of the house, away from views of this terrace. By my reckoning, then, if anyone had seen what had happened to Wanda Harper, it was most likely one of my fellow authors.

Now I needed to find out who was in which room and who might have been in his or her room when the murder occurred.

Nodding at the PC, I turned and walked back toward the door through which I had come out onto the terrace. Then, struck by a memory, I paused.

Norah Tattersall had said she saw Giles arguing with Wanda Harper on the terrace. Where had she been when she saw this? Had she been in her room?

I flashed back to an earlier memory, my first meeting with her. She had come down the hall after Giles and I had just met Isabella Veryan and George Austen-Hare. Most likely, she had come from her own room, which meant that she, too, was in the same wing with us. Interesting, I thought, that Lady Hermione should have quartered Norah Tattersall there rather than with the other aspiring writers in the other wing.

I resumed my progress toward the door. Once inside the house, I averted my eyes from the atrocious furnishings of the room as I crossed it. Out in the hall, I sought out a phone. I wanted to consult Lady Hermione's butler, Dingleby, to discern whether he would supply the information I wanted.

I found a phone on a table in the hall, and I examined it. Beside the phone was a list of extensions within the house, and I punched in the number for the butler's pantry. Moments later, Dingleby came on the line.

In response to my request, he said he would be with me in a few moments' time, in my room.

Proceeding to my room, I was relieved not to encounter anyone on the way. Giles was busy in his room, tapping away at his laptop computer, and he waved a hand to acknowledge my presence. I went into the bathroom, realizing that it was time for one of my pills, while I waited for Dingleby.

I had just sat down in one of the hideous but oddly comfortable chairs when a knock sounded at the door. "Enter!"

The door opened, and Dingleby stepped in, carefully closing it behind him.

"Yes, Dr. Kirby-Jones? How might I be of assistance?"

He really was the most peculiar-looking butler I had ever seen, but now was not the time to speculate upon such an incongruity. "Yes, Dingleby, I was wondering whether you might be able to assist me with some information."

"Yes, sir. I'd be most delighted to oblige, if I can." He waited, his face blank, his attitude patient.

"Could you tell me, Dingleby, which of my fellow guests have rooms whose windows look out upon the terrace?"

A small frown creased Dingleby's face as he considered my request. Evidently, he could find no reason not to provide the information, for he soon spoke. "That's easy enough, sir. All the other writers have rooms that look out upon the terrace. You are the only one of them on this side of the hall."

"Thank you, Dingleby."

He nodded, then asked, "Would there be anything else, Dr. Kirby-Jones?"

"Two more questions," I said.

He waited.

"What about Miss Tattersall?"

"She, too, is on that side of the hall." He was too well trained to prompt me for the second question.

"Finally, Dingleby, I wondered whether you could tell me exactly which room each of them is in."

He frowned at that, but once again, I suppose he could discern no reason not to answer me.

"Certainly, sir. Dame Isabella Veryan is in the first room, followed by Mr. Austen-Hare. Next is Miss Putney, and then Mr. Harbaugh. Miss Tattersall has the last room on that side. Mr. Dunn is in the other wing."

I stood. "Thank you, Dingleby. You've been most helpful. I appreciate the information."

He bowed. "Then, sir, if that is all?"

"Yes, thank you."

He turned and left, closing the door quietly behind him.

Giles came out of his room. "What was all that about?"

"I wanted to verify something," I said.

Giles thought for a moment. "You wanted to know whether any of your fellow writers, and Miss Tattersall, could have seen something on the terrace from their rooms."

"Exactly."

"It now occurs to me," Giles said, "that we never ascertained just where Miss Tattersall was when she spied me having my little argument with Wanda Harper."

"Exactly," I repeated. "And I think I shall just step along to her room and talk to her about that—if she's in, of course."

"Good idea," Giles said. He stretched and rolled his neck. "Better you than me."

"Why don't you take a break?"

"Another good idea," he said. "I think I might go out and take a brisk walk, clear my head a little." He walked over to the window and looked outside. "And it's not raining at the moment."

I followed him out in the hall and headed one way while he went the other, toward the stairs. I walked down the hall until I had come to the last door on the side of the wing facing the terrace. Pausing in front of the door I hoped belonged to Norah Tattersall, I knocked and waited.

No response.

I knocked again.

Still no response. Sighing in exasperation, I was about to turn and walk back down the hall to my own room, when I spotted a small triangle of white sticking out from under the door.

Extracting a pen from my pocket, I bent down and placed the tip of the pen cover on the paper and teased it out from under the door. I was being terribly nosy, but with a murderer loose in Kinsale House, I wasn't too worried about the niceties at this point.

I squatted and examined what I had pulled from underneath the door. It was a piece of paper, folded in half. The initials *N. T.* were printed on the side facing up at me. Again using the pen, I maneuvered the point inside the fold and managed to open the note.

Printed on the page were the words *KEEP YOUR MOUTH SHUT.*

Chapter Seventeen

I stared at the words for a moment longer; then I folded the paper with care and slid it back under Norah Tattersall's door. I stood up.

Someone else—the killer, perhaps?—had figured out that Norah might have seen something she shouldn't have out on that terrace.

That was one possible scenario.

A second one came to mind. Perhaps one of my fellow authors, knowing that Norah was aware of his or her dirty little secret, was simply warning her not to talk about it.

Either way, Norah Tattersall probably knew something that might help get this mess resolved.

But where is Norah? I wondered as I walked back down the hall toward my own room.

As I closed the door of my room behind me, I dismissed the notion that I should have kept the note to show to Robin Chase. For one thing, I didn't want to face a lecture on my interference with his investigation. Better to let Norah find it, I thought, then try to accost her shortly afterward and question her.

In order to make that ploy work, though, I had to find Norah. To that end, I picked up the telephone and punched in the number for the admirable Dingleby's extension. It was not Dingleby who answered, however. Another servant, who failed to identify herself, took my request to locate Miss Tattersall and send her to my room.

While waiting for Norah Tattersall to appear at my door, I busied myself with finishing some of the notes I wanted to make on a couple of the more promising manuscripts I had read. About fifteen minutes after I had called downstairs, I heard a knock on my door.

"Enter," I called.

The door opened, and Norah Tattersall stuck her head in. "You were looking for me?" She hesitated in the doorway.

"Yes, Miss Tattersall," I said in my most charming tones. "I apologize for summoning you in this manner, but I had a request to make of you."

She pushed the door farther open and took a step inside the room. She wouldn't come all the way in, and she kept casting furtive glances over her shoulder, as if someone were at her back.

"What do you want?" Her tone was brusque to the point of rudeness. Given the scene earlier in the day with Giles, I couldn't blame her attitude, though it wouldn't be of much help in getting me what I wanted.

I had an idea, though, how to get her to lower her guard. "Miss Tattersall, I've read the portion of the manuscript you submitted, and I wondered whether you have a bit more of it with you that I could read."

"You want to read *more* of it?" The sheer incredulity in her voice almost gave me pause at the thought that I was going to be raising her hopes falsely. No doubt I was the first person in quite some time who actually wanted to read more of her horrible work.

I made the not terribly difficult decision to quash my finer feelings as I nodded. "If that wouldn't be too much trouble."

"Certainly not," she said, her face lighting up with pleasure. "I'll be right back."

"Shall I come with you? No need for you to have to traipse back here."

She was too excited at the thought of my reading more of her work to think about the oddity of my going with her, since my room was nearer the stairs than hers. She practically ran out of the room, and I made haste to follow her.

I was right on her heels as she paused to open her door. She stepped inside, putting one foot square in the middle of the folded paper lying on the floor. In her excitement she didn't seem to have noticed it. I coughed and drew her attention to it.

Norah stared blankly down at the paper. "What's this, I wonder."

She stooped over to retrieve it, unfolding it as she straightened up. Her lips moved as she read the words. The color drained from her face.

She crumpled the paper in her hands and moved jerkily away from the door, toward one of the chairs in the room.

"What's the matter, Miss Tattersall? Is it bad news

of some kind?" I came and squatted beside her chair. "Is there anything I can do?"

Mutely she shook her head. I held out a hand toward the paper balled up in her fist. Her fingers tightened around it as she realized what I was trying to do.

"Nothing you need concern yourself with, Dr. Kirby-Jones," she said, attempting a firm tone and failing.

"You look like you've had a shock, Miss Tattersall. Are you certain there isn't something I can do for you?" I stood up, gazing down at her with an earnest expression of helpfulness on my face. "Perhaps I should ring for some hot tea?"

"No, just someone's attempt at a joke," she responded, her voice less tremulous.

"It's a trifle close in here, don't you think?" I said, striding away from her, toward one of the windows overlooking the terrace.

"I beg your pardon?" she said.

"Perhaps if we could open one of these windows," I said, bracingly cheerful. "The fresh air would perk you up."

She said nothing more, just continued to look at me oddly. I made an effort at opening one of the windows but gave up quickly. Then I turned to her, as if struck by a new notion. "Your window overlooks the terrace."

"Yes," she said, puzzled.

"You must have been here, looking down on the terrace, when you saw my assistant arguing with Miss Harper."

As she stared at me, the color once again drained from her face. Her mouth opened and closed several times, but no sound came out.

"Was it from here that you saw them talking?" I said, coming to crouch beside her chair again.

She gazed into my face, and I could feel the fear emanating from her. "Yes, I suppose I must have been," she finally said, though she did it unwillingly.

"Then perhaps you saw someone else talking to Miss Harper," I said. "After, of course, Giles had left her?"

I made it a question. She licked her lips with her tongue, and her breath was coming in short gasps.

"Did you see someone else, Miss Tattersall?"

She nodded.

"When?"

"Before." She stumbled over the word. "Not after."

I frowned. This wasn't going to help much, but I also thought she might be lying to me about the "before."

"Who was it?" I asked.

She swallowed. "I can't say."

"You didn't recognize the person?" My tone scoffed at the idea.

She just sat there and stared at me. She knew perfectly well whom she had seen, but she wasn't going to tell me. Her hand tightened convulsively around the threatening note.

"Very well, Miss Tattersall," I said, standing up. "But if you won't talk to me, then you'd better go downstairs right now and talk to Detective Inspector Chase. You could be shielding the murderer."

She drew back at that, her eyes blinking rapidly.

"Don't be foolish," I said as gently as I could. "Are you certain you don't want to confide in me?"

"No! I mean, yes!"

"So be it," I said. Foolish, stubborn woman! She was well on her way to becoming corpse number two. "Think about what I said, about talking to the police. For your own safety, if nothing else."

I got no further response from her, and so I went out the door, shutting it none too gently behind me.

Of all the aggravating, impossible, stubborn women! I shook my head over Norah Tattersall's intransigent stupidity as I strode down the hall toward my room. Unless she told Robin what—or more important, whom—she had seen, and right away, she could be putting herself in danger. I wondered whom she was protecting.

One possible answer occurred to me as I thought quickly back over some of the events of the past two days. Might as well kill two birds, and all that.

I paused near the end of the hallway and looked at the doors across the passageway from my own door, keeping in mind what Dingleby had told me. Then I stepped up to the door that I thought belonged to George Austen-Hare and knocked briskly.

"Who is it?" I heard him call.

"Kirby-Jones," I responded.

I heard some shuffling about inside, and moments later the door opened. George stared at me, his face blank of expression.

"Could I speak with you for a moment, George?" I smiled disarmingly.

He shrugged and stood aside. Taking that as an invitation, I walked past him into the room. A quick glance around assured me that this chamber was just as appallingly decorated as my own, with an abundance of maroon velvet and gold trimmings.

George motioned toward a chair, one of a pair near one of the windows. I sat down, and he seated himself opposite me.

He still hadn't spoken, and I took a quick moment to examine him. He didn't seem at all frightened. Wary, if anything. I doubted he suspected me of being a murderer, but he didn't quite trust me.

"I need your advice, George," I said, attempting to look as if I might be at my wits' end. I twisted my hands in dramatic fashion. "What am I going to do about Norah Tattersall?"

His eyes widened. "What d'ye mean, Simon? What's Norah done now?"

I glanced away, as if I were embarrassed to look him straight in the eye. "It's not so much what she's *done*, George." I pretended to take a deep breath, and I could feel his apprehension coming to the fore.

"What has she said?" George's hands tightened on the arms of his chair.

"I thought I had better consult you, George," I said, still not looking at him, "because, well, because you seem to have known her for quite some time. And also because Norah seems to be rather *fond* of you." I did my best to load that one word with as much suggestive significance as I could.

I risked glancing at George's face, and it was slowly suffusing with red. I was on to something here, as I had suspected I might be.

"I rather got the idea," I continued, "that you and she had, um, well, that you had had a relationship that was, shall we say, a bit warm?"

"Blast the woman!" George said gruffly. "Can't ever keep her business to herself, nor mine either!"

That's what a little fishing will get you, I thought in satisfaction. "Not everyone can be discreet, George," I said sadly. "But I can assure you that I will be."

He harrumphed at that. "A feller makes mistakes

sometimes, Simon, and demmed if they don't come back to haunt him."

"Like Norah?" I said in a jocular, man-of-the-world tone.

George nodded emphatically. "Man in my position gets approached all the time. Because of my books, you see. Women get the idea that I'm like one of the heroes in my books. They just throw themselves at me sometimes."

"And Norah did that, too?"

"Made no secret of it, first time I met her, a few years ago here at Kinsale House." George snorted in derision. "Like a cat in season, she was. Took me a bit longer than it should have to see that she wanted me to help her with that blasted book of hers as much as anything."

I shook my head in sympathy. "Amazing what some will try, just to get published, isn't it?"

George shifted uncomfortably in his chair. "Shouldn't have gotten involved with her, no doubt about that. But she was so demmed admiring, acted like I'd hung the moon and the stars, and all that rot!" The self-mockery in his voice was plain.

"It appears to me that she still has feelings for you, George."

"She keeps pestering me," George admitted, "even though I broke it off with her two years ago. And she keeps trotting out that manuscript, waving it at me."

"I guess she hasn't quite given up on you, George." I winked at him, and he blushed. "Though I got the distinct impression you hadn't let the grass grow under your feet, once she was out of the picture. If you know what I mean." I grinned broadly.

The color drained from his face. "You shouldn't

listen to Norah, Simon. No telling what she'd say, if she'd a mind to."

"Really, George?" I stared at him, my eyebrows quirked up. "Sounded rather plausible to me, I must say. Even though it might not look good for you."

That was a stab in the dark, but nothing ventured, nothing gained.

George stood up, radiating anger. "I didn't kill that silly woman, no matter what Norah may have told you about my relationship with her!"

Chapter Eighteen

George might have taken it amiss if I patted myself on the back at this point, but I allowed myself a small smile of satisfaction. I had thought he might be the easiest to nudge, shall we say, into confiding in me, and it seemed as if I had read him correctly.

"No one's accusing you of murdering her, George," I said, and he began to relax. "Yet."

His eyes widened as I added that last word. He began to babble so fast, I couldn't make out what he was saying, and I held up a hand to shush him.

"I'm certain, George, that it can't be as bad as all that. First, and simplest, just answer this: do you have an alibi for this afternoon, when someone killed her?"

Miserable, George shook his head "no."

"I'll bet you were here, in your room alone, weren't you?" I asked. He nodded.

"Ah, that's too bad, George," I said with grave concern. "I'm just thrilled as I can be, let me tell you, that I was in plain sight of several people during the time when Ms. Harper managed to get herself killed." I laughed in self-deprecation. "Otherwise, I know who'd be number one on the hit parade of suspects!"

George managed a weak smile at that sally before I continued. "But enough of my ill-placed humor, George. We should concentrate on exonerating *you*." He nodded, his head bobbing up and down like a Ping-Pong ball.

"Now, I didn't get very many details from Norah," I said. That much was certainly true, since Norah hadn't given me *any* details of George's affair with the late unlamented. "And you don't have to share every little bit with me, George." He smiled wanly at that. "But if we're going to make sure you're out of this, we have to sort out *why* you'd have wanted to murder her in the first place. Surely an *affaire du coeur* gone sour wouldn't be enough reason?"

George pulled a handkerchief from his pants pocket and began to mop his suddenly febrile brow with it. "Afraid it's not that simple, Simon. Not that simple at all."

"My dear George, whatever do you mean?" I leaned forward slightly in my chair, as if I were hanging on his every word. Which, naturally, I was, since I figured we were about to get to the really good dirt.

"Wasn't an affair of the heart, so much as affair of the loins." George uttered the words in tones of disgust, yet he couldn't help the salaciously reminiscent smile hanging on his lips. "Woman was like a panther. Never satisfied, always wanting more."

Then he looked embarrassed at having admitted that to me.

I laughed, deep from my chest. "But you were certainly man enough for her, I'm sure, George."

He preened a bit at that. He really fancied himself as a ladies' man. And, for all I knew, he really was. He was famous, wealthy, and not totally devoid of attractions. Some women no doubt actually liked the garden-gnome type.

"How did you meet her, George?"

"Through Nina," George said, his brow furrowing. "Had no idea at the time, naturally, that it was a put-up job between the two of them. Wanda was working for Nina, but I didn't know that."

I sat back in my chair, hands steepled, chin propped on forefingers. "Aha! I thought I saw the hand of Lady Machiavelli in all of this."

George laughed, the first sound of pure amusement since I had come into his room. "Good name for the wench! Nina could have taught Signor Niccolò a thing or two."

This wasn't moving along quite as fast as I'd like, so I decided to nudge him into a higher gear. "So Wanda entrapped you in some kind of compromising situation, I take it?"

His face turned an alarming shade of red, and I was on the point of suggesting I ring for a shot of whiskey when his eyes stopped popping and his breathing slowed down to a near-normal rate again. "Told you she was never satisfied, right? Always wanted to be trying something new and different. 'Adventurous,' she called herself. Fool that I was, I went along with her." He shuddered. "Though I suppose I ought to have known better."

"And someone walked in on you?" I didn't have

to pretend to be mortified for his sake. He had clearly been led into a rather nasty trap.

"Not precisely," George said, then took a deep breath before he could force himself to continue. "Someone taking a video of us without my knowledge."

"Oh, dear," I said. "And I suppose they—meaning Nina, chiefly, of course—threatened to embarrass you with it."

George nodded miserably.

I could just imagine the headlines in the scandal sheets here, all about how the noted best-selling author of romantic fiction liked kinky sex. George would become a laughingstock. His sales would probably go through the roof, but he'd be too embarrassed to show his face in public again.

"Poor George," I said in total and sincere sympathy. Until these past few days at Kinsale House, I had thought Nina possessed the usual share of ethics, but evidently I was wrong.

I was nevertheless puzzled about something. "Why, George? I mean, why would Nina go to these lengths to put a client in her control like this?"

"She's power-mad," George said. "The ultimate control freak. Wants you to do everything her way, and the better you sell, the more she wants out of you. Once she signs you, she doesn't want to let you go."

"She's totally round the bend, isn't she?" I said, my voice calm, but inside I was, I'll admit, freaking out just a bit. I, of all people, couldn't afford an agent like this. If she ever got an inkling of the truth about me, no telling what she'd try to do with the knowledge.

I might have to kill her myself.

No, I shouldn't even joke about something like

that. A vampire following the old ways might not hesitate to get rid of someone like Nina who posed such an obvious threat. But I had most definitely not chosen the old ways when I became a vampire. I was one of the new, kinder, gentler breed of vampires, happy with the little pills that made biting people on the neck and draining them of blood a relic of the past.

Enough of that; back to the matter at hand. I had manipulated George fairly easily into telling me what I wanted to know, at least as far as it concerned him and his potential motive for murder. But would he prove as easy to manipulate when it came to digging up dirt on his fellow suspects?

I flashed back on something Nina had done earlier, and that gave me an idea.

"Tell me, George, what was that earlier today, with Nina and Dexter Harbaugh and that bit about the spider?" I laughed. "I thought Dexter was going to jump out of his skin."

George shifted uneasily in his chair, even while he attempted to hide a grin. "I really shouldn't be telling you this, Simon. I really shouldn't." His mouth closed in a prim line, but he was simply waiting for me to encourage him.

"Come, now, George, you can't stop now! There's obviously a good story to be told."

"Dexter would be simply livid if he knew I'd told you, so you must promise not to breathe a word of it. Not a word!"

"Of course, George, I wouldn't dream of it," I assured him. "Except, naturally, if it turns out that Dexter is the murderer."

"Fair enough, Simon, fair enough!" His mouth split in a huge grin. "Man's terrified of spiders. Can you believe it?"

I had to laugh. "I figured as much. Nina wouldn't have said what she did if she hadn't known he'd react in that way."

George nodded emphatically. "Yes! Not only spiders, Simon! Not just spiders. Dexter is afraid of the dark. Has to have a light on at night, or he can't sleep."

"Really?" I said. "How on earth did you find out that little bit of information?"

George flushed at the implication he thought he read in my words. "Had to share quarters at a conference with him once, years ago, before either of us became very well known. Insisted a light be left on all night. Got him to admit to me he was afraid of the dark."

I threw back my head and laughed. "I can see the headlines now. 'Tough-guy writer needs nightlight.' The press would have a field day with that one, not to mention the bit about the spiders. No wonder he makes his heroes so tough."

George nodded. "Exactly. Who'd buy the books if they thought the author was a nancy-boy?"

I shot him a look at that one, and to his credit, he flushed and muttered, "Sorry. Didn't mean it like it sounded."

I decided to overlook it and move on.

"Okay, so Nina knows about ol' Dex's phobias. She could easily use that to manipulate him, keep him under her thumb. But I don't see any connection between Dexter and Wanda Harper."

I stared at George expectantly. He squirmed again in his chair.

He remained quiet, though I could sense he was bursting to tell me something.

"Okay, George, spill it!" I smiled to encourage him.

"Don't know for sure," he said at last. He focused his eyes on the floor. "Suspect, though, that Nina has a video of Dexter and that woman. Probably chasing him around the room with a spider. Screaming his head off like an old woman." Then he couldn't keep himself from laughing aloud at the thought of that.

I joined him. The vision of tough-guy Dexter Harbaugh being chased by a spider-wielding Wanda Harper *was* funny, even if it was cruel. The man was so obnoxious, I couldn't help enjoying the thought of him cut down to size.

If I were Dexter Harbaugh, however, that could be humiliating enough to make me want to kill.

I figured he had the motive, if Nina was twisting the screws hard and he decided he'd had enough. But did he have the opportunity?

More digging was on the agenda, definitely. If George really had been in his room during the time when Wanda Harper met her killer out on the terrace, he wouldn't be able to tell me about anyone else's whereabouts at the time. It wouldn't hurt to ask, though.

"Did you see, or hear, anyone else during the time that the murder must have occurred, George?"

Earlier, when he had told me he was here in this room when the murder took place, George hadn't given off the vibes that would have told me he was lying. If he was clever enough, and cold enough, he could mask the emotions to keep me from feeling the truth. Now I could sense some hesitation in him. Was he about to lie to me? Or did he simply not want to tell me something?

Chapter Nineteen

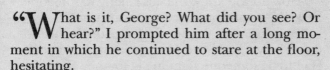

"What is it, George? What did you see? Or hear?" I prompted him after a long moment in which he continued to stare at the floor, hesitating.

Finally, he raised his eyes to meet mine. "Did see something."

"On the terrace?" This was like pulling teeth. "What did you see, George? Or whom?"

He stared unhappily at me, stuck in debate with himself.

"George," I said as gently as I could, given the frustration I was now feeling, "it will have to come out. You'll have to tell the police."

"Suppose you're right, Simon, but I don't think they'll find it all that helpful," he said, then took a deep breath. "Looked out the window at one point, thinking about taking a walk, and saw the Harper creature on the terrace. Talking to someone."

"Who, George?"

He shrugged. "Not sure. Let me show you." He stood up and walked to the window, drawing the curtain aside.

Standing beside him, I gazed down upon the terrace. I could see the lonely PC still at his place, guarding the scene of the crime. He was having a furtive smoke, lounging near the balustrade where someone had pushed the cement pot off on Wanda Harper.

"She was standing right about there," George said, "talking to someone on the ground."

"About where the PC is?" I asked to clarify. George nodded.

I looked again. From this angle, someone standing on the ground close to the terrace wall couldn't be seen from George's window.

"How do you know she was talking to someone?" I asked. "If you couldn't see anyone else?"

"Poor creature was leaning over the balustrade, that's how. Could see her gesturing at someone. Had to be someone standing below her. She was in the way of my seeing just who it was."

"How long were you at the window?"

"Only a moment," George said. "Weather looked too iffy, so I decided against a walk. Besides"—he shifted uncomfortably—"didn't want to run into that creature outside. Or anywhere else."

"You didn't see anything distinguishable about the person? The top of the head, perhaps, or a glimpse of the clothing?"

"Nothing," he said. He let the curtain drop and went back to his chair.

I followed him but didn't sit down again. "Pity that you didn't see who it was, George." I was thinking, however, that it could have been Giles, but if it was,

I reasoned, how could Norah Tattersall have seen him? She was much farther along the hall than George, and her angle of view down upon the terrace would be different, of course. But could she have seen from her window whoever was on the ground? Or would the terrace wall have shielded that person from view?

Perhaps Norah hadn't really been in her room when she saw Giles arguing with Wanda Harper, I reasoned. Maybe instead, she was outside on the grounds somewhere. What was it she had said to me when I had asked her if she had seen Wanda and Giles from her window? *"Yes, I suppose I must have been."*

That made me suppose that I had led my witness unintentionally. Norah hadn't said she had been in her room when she had seen Wanda and Giles. Instead, she had responded more conditionally, and at the time I hadn't really paid attention to exactly what she had said.

I had been wrapped up in my thoughts, so much so that I had forgotten George for the moment. Now I saw that he was eyeing me uneasily. I flashed him a reassuring smile.

"Not to worry, George, just ruminating over things," I said.

"Playing Sherlock, eh, Simon?" George laughed.

"Perhaps, George. You must admit it's tempting."

George shrugged in response. I offered him my hand, and he took it. We shook. "Thanks, George. I appreciate your candor, and I assure you that what you told me earlier will go no further unless it's absolutely necessary."

"Thank you, Simon," he said, standing and following me to the door. "I didn't kill that woman, but I can't say that I can condemn the poor sod who did."

"I can understand that, George," I said. "Promise me, though, you will inform the police of what you saw on the terrace."

After assuring me that he would, George shut the door firmly behind me. I went back to my room, hoping that Giles had returned from his walk.

Not only had he returned, I discovered when I entered my room, he was reclining comfortably on my bed, snoring.

"Giles! Wake up." I shook him none too gently.

His first indignant cry died upon his lips, which quickly curved into an inviting grin when he realized who had accosted him. "There's plenty of room here, Simon, if you'd like to climb in."

I shook my head at him. "Nice try, Giles." I retreated from the bed and sat down in one of the chairs near the window. I watched as he sat up on the bed and ran a hand through his hair. He yawned and swung his feet to the floor. Thankfully, he hadn't removed his clothing, only his shoes, before making himself so comfortable on my bed. He padded over to the other chair and plopped down in it, regarding me with a disappointed smile.

"You rang?" he said.

"Tell me what happened when you argued with Wanda Harper on the terrace."

"Not much, frankly," Giles said, his face expressing his curiosity. "I told her I knew who she really was, and she wanted to know how." He laughed. "I told her she really ought to lock her room if she didn't want people finding out her secrets, and she got rather angry at that. She had quite an impressive vocabulary of vulgar words, that woman."

I nodded. "Yes, I found that out myself."

Giles shrugged. "And that was about it. I listened to her cursing at me for a moment; then I told her she could call me all the names she wanted to, but it wouldn't change the outcome of what would happen as soon as Lady Hermione knew the truth. Then she uttered one more vulgarity and flounced off down the terrace. That was the last I saw of her, because I came back inside then."

"You were on the terrace, then, when you confronted her?"

Giles nodded. "Yes, when I went out onto the terrace, she was only a few feet away from me, as if she had just arrived there herself. Why do you ask?"

"Because George Austen-Hare saw her arguing with someone, but she was at that point by the balustrade, and the other person was standing on the ground below the terrace wall."

Giles considered that for a moment. "Most likely, that was after I saw her. Unfortunately for me, I didn't see anyone else on the terrace with her." He breathed a deep sigh of relief. "Maybe that will give Chase something else to do."

"Giles, you don't really think he considers you a viable suspect, do you?" My tone was light and mocking.

His eyes darkened for a moment. "Maybe not. But he doesn't really care for me, Simon. Surely you've picked up on that."

"I've noticed that you're none too friendly with him, Giles, but to be truthful, I thought that was more on your part than his."

"Because you think I'm jealous of him, is that it, Simon?" Giles laughed.

"Why would you be jealous of him, Giles?" I countered playfully. "You're young, handsome, titled, reasonably well off."

"Because of the way you look at him, Simon. He's aware of it, I can assure you, though he pretends otherwise." Giles's temper was becoming increasingly strained.

I'm not averse to having two attractive men fighting over me, mind you, but I thought I'd better take control of this situation before it got out of hand.

"Giles, look at me," I said gently, waiting for him to do as I asked. His eyes stared straight into mine, and for the first time I saw the vulnerability and uncertainty there. Maybe his feelings for me were genuine after all, more mature and deeper than I had reckoned. He was so casually flirtatious on a daily basis that I had often been inclined to dismiss his feelings as simple lust and nothing more. But perhaps I had been misreading him all along.

"I like flirting as much as the next man," I said, "and I'll admit to flirting with Robin Chase. It's amusing, and I get a kick out of it. But I don't have a professional relationship with him. I lose nothing by being playful with him and watching him squirm ever so slightly."

"Where does that leave me?" Giles said, and to his credit he managed not to sound self-pitying.

"I value your friendship, and I value our working relationship," I said, and I could see him relax. "You've been very good for me, Giles, and you've made my working life much easier, I must say."

"And is that all I am to you, Simon? A friend and assistant?" His voice was soft, and he had turned away from me.

If I had told him he was also a constant temptation, he would have read the wrong things into the admission, so I stilled the impulse to utter the words.

"Those are both things I value very much, Giles,"

I said, "and I know you want more from me than that. For now, though, I think it's better for both of us to be content with the present situation. We have plenty of time to see what might develop, don't we?"

He turned to face me again, his eyes shining with both hope and longing. "Oh, Simon, what choice do I have?"

I wasn't ready yet to tell him all my secrets, or face the responsibilities that the kind of relationship he wanted would entail. He might never want to see me again, or, worse, he might be so horrified that he would reveal the truth of what I was to everyone around us. Then my existence would be sheer hell. I liked what I had found in Snupperton Mumsley, and I didn't want to lose it. I had to know him better, feel more confident in his feelings for me and mine for him, before I could take such an irrevocable step.

I smiled to take the sting out of the words. "Then I guess we're stuck with each other for a while, eh?"

He grinned. "You won't get rid of me very easily, Simon; I can promise you that."

"I hope not, Giles, I hope not," I said softly.

Giles got up from the chair and retrieved his shoes from the bedside. As he sat down on the bed to put his shoes back on, he asked, "What are we going to do next, Simon?"

"I think another talk with Norah Tattersall is in order. She most certainly knows more than she's telling, and I want to see if I can persuade her to tell me what she knows. That is, if she hasn't already told it all to Robin."

"He certainly won't tell you, Simon," Giles said, his face split in a huge grin.

"No, he wouldn't," I conceded. "I'll just have to tackle Norah anyway." I got up from my chair. "While I do that, you keep digging for more dirt. Someone in this place had a motive for murder, and we need to find out what it is."

Giles mumbled something in response as I went out the door. I moved quickly down the hall to Norah Tattersall's room, hoping that I would be lucky enough to find her on the first try.

I knocked firmly on the door—so firmly, in fact, that I pushed it open slightly. It hadn't been securely closed. I pushed the door open a bit farther. "Norah! Miss Tattersall!" I called. "May I come in?"

No one answered me, but made curious by the fact that the door had been open, I went on inside her room.

There I got a bit of a shock. Norah Tattersall was in the room, after all, but she was very, very dead.

Chapter Twenty

Someone had made cruel use of a beautiful silk scarf by wrapping it around Norah Tattersall's neck and squeezing until the poor woman strangled to death.

Not a pretty sight, I observed as I stared at the corpse. Death and the dead hold few terrors for someone like me—one advantage of being dead yourself. But the stupidity of Norah Tattersall's death angered me. If the silly cow had confided in me, or better yet, in the police, she wouldn't have come to this.

I had no idea what she had hoped to gain by withholding what she knew, but it was certainly not this, a painful and terrifying death.

I stepped closer to the corpse, pausing within about two feet of the chair in which it sat. The head lolled back obscenely, and the arms hung down loosely over the arms of the chair. I walked slowly around the chair, taking care not to get too close.

Nothing. I could see nothing that would be a possible clue to the identity of the murderer. The scarf that had been used as a garrotte was silk and patterned in rich, vibrant colors. Most likely, it was one of Norah's own. I frowned, thinking back to the last time I had seen her. Had she been wearing it then? I didn't think so. The police could find out where it came from, no doubt.

Thinking of the police recalled me to my duty. I didn't relish the thought of having to tell Robin Chase that I had another murder victim for him, but I couldn't leave the body for someone else to find. I left the door open, not wanting to disturb possible evidence any more than I already had, and ran back down the hall to my room.

I grabbed up the phone and punched in the number of Dingleby's extension, completely ignoring Giles's attempt to claim my attention.

Dingleby answered after a couple of rings, and I quickly explained what had happened. He would have Detective Inspector Chase on the scene as quickly as possible, he affirmed. I put the phone back in its cradle and turned to regard Giles in the act of collapsing into a chair.

"Good heavens, Simon," he sputtered. *"Another* murder!"

"No time to talk now, Giles," I said, heading out the door once again. "No, stay here," I ordered as he made a move to follow me.

I wanted to get back to the door of Norah Tattersall's room to keep anyone else from discovering what I had until the police arrived. I hadn't been at my post for more than about three minutes when

I looked down the hall to see Robin Chase, followed by a number of his team, moving rapidly toward me.

As they reached me, I stood aside and gestured into the room with my left hand. Robin gave me an exasperated look as he preceded his team into the room. I waited in the hall for perhaps five minutes before Robin joined me there. Over his shoulder I could see his team begin their grim job.

Robin took my arm and guided me a few paces down the hall. "Would you care to explain to me, Simon," Robin said, "how you came to find yet another corpse?"

I resisted the urge to respond with something facetious; now was not the time for my quirky sense of humor. "I simply knocked on her door, Robin, and the door began moving inward. Obviously, it hadn't been shut completely. I called out her name, and when I got no response, I pushed the door open farther and came into the room. And then I saw, very quickly, why she hadn't answered me."

"Why did you want to talk to her?"

"Because I was afraid something like this would happen," I said.

"And why would you think that?" Robin's skepticism was evident in his tone.

"I had spoken with her earlier, right after she found a threatening note in her room. It was fairly obvious to me that she had seen something to do with the first murder, but she wouldn't tell me what she had seen."

"What did this threatening note say?" Robin said. "Did you see it?"

Feeling a bit like the proverbial cat caught with his nose in the cream, I told Robin how I had found the note and read it. The corners of his mouth quirked up a bit as he listened, but otherwise he did not acknowledge my snooping.

"What did she do with the note?"

"She crumpled it up, and after that I don't know what she did with it. You might find it in her room," I said.

"Right. Please wait here a moment." He left me to instruct the men working the crime scene and was back before I had much time to think about how best to tell him the rest of what I had learned, from both the victim and George Austen-Hare.

"I think perhaps we had better continue our interview downstairs, Simon," Robin said, taking me by the arm and guiding me down the hall, toward the stairs.

"Certainly, Robin," I said, following him. Neither of us said anything more until we were seated in the room where he had interviewed Giles and me earlier. As he sat down, Robin motioned for the PC who had remained on duty in the room to sit and take notes.

"Right, Dr. Kirby-Jones," Robin said, all at once more formal in the presence of a subordinate, "you were telling me how you had spoken earlier in the day to the victim."

"Yes, Detective Inspector Chase," I said, proceeding to give him a report of my conversation with Norah. I placed particular emphasis on the words Norah had used in answering my question about whether she had seen Wanda Harper's argument with Giles from her bedroom window.

Robin waited until I had finished before he fastened upon the point that I had wanted him to grasp. "You believe she may not have been in her bedroom, then, when she witnessed the argument between the first victim and Sir Giles Blitherington?"

"I'm beginning to believe so, yes," I said. "Tell me, have you spoken with George Austen-Hare in the last hour or so?"

"As a matter of fact, I have," Robin admitted, his eyes alight with curiosity, "but naturally I can't reveal what it was he told me."

"Of course not," I said, flashing Robin one of my most dazzling smiles. He blinked, then began to finger his mustache nervously. "But if he has talked to you, then perhaps what I have to tell you next won't come as a surprise."

"Proceed," Robin said, making an effort to leave his mustache alone.

I reiterated what George had told me about seeing Wanda Harper conversing with someone on the terrace, then offered Robin the opinion that Norah might have seen who it was. "If she was, as I suspect," I concluded with a flourish, "not in her room but somewhere on the grounds with a good view of what was going on there at the front of the terrace."

"It's certainly possible," Robin allowed. "And I suppose you're thinking that Miss Tattersall approached whomever she had seen with the intention of using that knowledge to her advantage?"

"I think it's very likely, don't you, Detective Inspector? Considering what has happened to Norah, I think it more than likely." I leaned back in my chair, very satisfied with my reasoning.

"The difficulty with that, Dr. Kirby-Jones, is that there seems little way of proving it."

"That, I'm afraid, is *your* job, Detective Inspector." I smiled sweetly as I said it, and Robin had to work to disguise his resulting laugh as a cough.

"It most certainly is, Dr. Kirby-Jones," Robin said when he had recovered himself. "And while I appreciate your willingness to be so very helpful in my investigation"—here he offered me a sardonic look—"I will remind you that this is a police matter and trust that you will do your best *not* to interfere any further."

Poor man, of course he had to say that, with one of his men listening. But if he thought I was going to stop being nosy, he really didn't know me very well. The twinkle in his eye as he stood to dismiss me made me think, however, that he did know me well enough.

"If you would be so kind, Dr. Kirby-Jones," Robin said, "as to go to the drawing room and wait for me there. I want to have everyone assembled there when I make the announcement about what has taken place. Please refrain from telling anyone else before I am ready to make the announcement."

"Certainly, Detective Inspector," I said, forbearing to mention that Giles already knew.

The drawing room was empty when I went in and found myself a comfortable chair, but in a few minutes my fellow writers began to trickle in. Lady Hermione came bustling in, attended as always by her silent shadow, Mary Monkley. Lady Hermione was fuming, none too discreetly, over what she viewed as Robin's rather peremptory summons. "What do you know about this, Dr. Kirby-Jones?" she barked at me.

"I'm afraid you'll have to wait for the Detective Inspector, Lady Hermione," I said. "I'm not at liberty to say anything at the moment."

She harrumphed at me. "Figures *you* would know what's going on." I could tell my stock was continuing to fall in Lady Hermione's eyes.

Surveying the assembled company, I figured

that Robin had asked only his cadre of suspects to attend this little briefing. None of the so-called students were here, only the instructors. And Giles, of course, as I acknowledged his entry into the room with a nod. He questioned me with his eyes, and I gave a slight shake of the head. He interpreted my gesture correctly, because he said nothing to the group about what he and I knew and they didn't.

Nina and her acolyte, Ashford Dunn, were the last of the suspects to enter the room. From their exchange of furtive smiles, I hazarded a guess as to how they had been occupying themselves when the summons had reached them. Really, Nina was too, too predictable in some ways. I sniffed in distaste. I couldn't sever my association with her quickly enough.

All eyes turned to the door as it opened to admit Robin Chase. He proceeded into the room, then halted at a point where he could see everyone.

"Lady Hermione, ladies, gentlemen, I regret to inform you that another murder has taken place."

A stunned silence followed his announcement; then a babble of remarks broke forth. The words all came so fast I couldn't take it all in, though I had hoped I might hear something that would betray the murderer.

Then Mary Monkley shrieked once and slid to the floor in a faint, diverting everyone's attention. Lady Hermione, however, appeared not to notice as the poor woman's head hit the rug with a faint thump. "This is an outrage!" Lady Hermione fumed, and the rafters shook. "How could you let something like this happen, Detective Inspector?"

While Lady Hermione raged in this vein, Isabella Veryan moved to kneel beside the stricken Mary

Monkley, chafing her hands and uttering soothing words. Slowly Miss Monkley revived, and Isabella assisted her into her chair.

Robin had flushed at Lady Hermione's onslaught. He was no doubt mortified that a second murder had taken place while he was still almost literally on the scene of the first murder, but he had no time now for recriminations. "I can assure you, Lady Hermione, everyone, that I deeply regret what has happened, but circumstances were somewhat beyond my control or that of my men."

"Just who was murdered, Detective Inspector?" Nina demanded.

"Stupid woman," Dexter Harbaugh said. "Look around you. Haven't you noticed who's not here?"

"Norah?" George Austen-Hare said in disbelief. "Was it Norah Tattersall?"

Robin inclined his head. "I'm afraid so. The body was discovered about twenty minutes ago. And now I must ask you all to remain here while I interview you, one by one, about your movements since I arrived here earlier in the day. And please, no talking amongst yourselves about any of this while you wait your turn." He motioned behind him for one of his men to move closer.

"Lady Hermione, if you please, I'd like to start with you," Robin said. He waited for Lady Hermione to rise from her seat, and he offered her his arm in a courtly gesture as she approached him. Her back stiff with outrage, she ignored his courtesy and stalked past him.

Robin followed her out of the room, and the door closed behind them. That left the rest of us in an uneasy silence, staring at one another, trying to figure out who among us was a double murderer.

Chapter Twenty-one

Dingleby brought a tea tray soon after Lady Hermione's departure, and for some time the only sounds in the room came from the slurping of tea or the clinking of spoons against the Kinsale china. Over the course of the next two hours, one by one the occupants of the room left, summoned by Robin Chase, until only I was left in the room. While we waited, no one had attempted to violate Robin's ban on conversation—not even Nina, much to my surprise.

Giles had been the next to last one called, and about fifteen minutes after his summons, one of Robin's men came to call me back into Robin's temporary office.

"Got the murderer pegged yet, Detective Inspector?" I asked as I made myself comfortable in the hot seat.

"You'll know the answer to that, Dr. Kirby-Jones,

just as soon as everyone else here at Kinsale House does," Robin said smoothly. "I'm sure you can appreciate the fact that I can't reveal any of the details of the investigation just now."

I rolled my eyes at Robin, but he affected not to notice. "For the sake of clarity, Dr. Kirby-Jones, I'd like to take you through your movements one more time, if you please."

Sighing at the tediousness of it all, I complied with Robin's request, making my answer as concise and brief as possible.

"An admirable summary, Dr. Kirby-Jones. Thank you for your continued cooperation," Robin said when I had finished.

"You're most welcome, Detective Inspector. I'm delighted to do what I can to assist you."

His head came up at that little sally, and he restrained a smile.

"I have asked everyone to remain tonight at Kinsale House, Dr. Kirby-Jones, and I will have members of the force posted throughout the house to ensure that there are no further incidents."

"What about tomorrow?" I inquired.

"After discussing the matter with Lady Hermione, I've decided that she may continue with her program if the participants are willing. However, anyone wishing to depart tomorrow may do so, after leaving suitable contact information with me or one of my staff."

I rose from my chair. "Thank you, Detective Inspector. And I do hope that your investigation is concluded swiftly."

Robin looked up from the desk. "So do I, Dr. Kirby-Jones. So do I." I could see that he was still smarting from the fact that a second murder had occurred practically under his nose. He had my sympathies, but he knew as well as I that there was little he could have done to prevent it, short of having each of us watched continuously by one of his men.

As I let myself out of the room, Robin was already on the phone, no doubt reporting to his superiors. I didn't envy him that call.

I encountered Dingleby in the hall, where he informed me that dinner was being served in the dining room, if I should choose to partake. Though I was tempted to follow him to the dining room—if for no other reason than to observe—I decided that I would rather spend the time in my room, mulling over the case and reading through what Giles had found through his researches.

In the upstairs hallway I found two of Robin's men posted on guard. One stood near the head of the stairs, another at the end of the corridor near Norah Tattersall's room. The lights in the hallway had been turned up to their brightest, and the two policemen would be able to see whenever anyone left his or her room during the night.

The small suite I shared with Giles was quiet when I entered. No doubt Giles was downstairs eating a belated meal with the others. I went into the bathroom and downed a pill, which was only a bit overdue. That task accomplished, I went into Giles's bedchamber and found the stack of file folders containing his researches from the Internet. Carrying them back into my room, I sat in my chair and began examining them. Giles, organized as ever, had already sorted everything by person, each folder neatly labeled so that I could see everything he had found, one person at a time.

I wasn't sure what to look for, other than some kind of link between Wanda Harper and one of the

suspects. It was possible that Giles could have uncovered some hint of the guilty secrets that my fellow writers were concealing, but the chances were,
their peccadilloes were beyond the reach of Giles's
computer.

I decided to start with Isabella Veryan. Though I
had a hard time seeing her in the role of a double
murderer, I had already observed enough about
her to sense that she most definitely was hiding
something. Something, moreover, that she did not
want her reading public to know. I recalled that
brief, emotion-laden scene with Lady Hermione.
Yes, they were both hiding something, but Lady Hermione would never give away her friend's secret.

The first document in Isabella's file was a brief
biography. I already knew about her aristocratic
lineage and her genteel upbringing. There were
details of her birth, education, and public service,
and a list of the awards she had won, not only for
her writing but also for various services to the com-
munity. On paper, she sounded boringly conven-
tional, other than the fact that she now made quite
a lucrative living writing about murder.

Next was the first in a series of interviews Giles
had found. Most of them were exceedingly dull,
the kind of interviews that every best-selling writer
grants, with the same boring questions. Isabella's
answers were pithy without sounding condescend-
ing, though I fancied I could read between the lines
to discern how distasteful she found the process.
Whenever the questions verged upon the personal,
straying from her writing, Isabella was firm but polite, refusing to be drawn. Isabella the writer came
through clearly, but little of the person behind the
writer.

How frustrating! There was something, somewhere, in Isabella's life that she was anxious to hide. Otherwise, Nina could not have blackmailed her.

I was about to lay Isabella's folder aside in disgust, even with documents left unread, when I found something a bit more promising. One of the tabloid papers had run a feature on Isabella and her family a few years ago, and at least one reporter had managed to dig up a bit of dirt from around the Veryan family tree.

Skimming rapidly, I learned that Isabella's cousin, the duke, had scandalized his family by running off from Cambridge with a chorus girl. Not to be outdone, one of that same duke's sisters had had a wild fling back during the Second World War with an avowed Nazi sympathizer. Other members of the extended family had done their best to stain the family escutcheon, but among them Isabella seemed to stand out as a model of virtue and propriety.

The reporter had, however, dug up the details of a romance between Isabella and an RAF pilot. He had been killed in a bombing raid over Germany, however, before the two could be married. Devastated by the loss, Isabella, according to one of her more disreputable cousins, had gone into seclusion for more than a year and had never expressed interest in another man after that. "If only the poor dear had been able to marry him and have a child," the cousin lamented, "how much happier poor dear Izzy might have been."

Izzy! Somehow I couldn't quite see Isabella Veryan as an "Izzy."

The cousin went on to lament how hard poor "Izzy" had worked after her year of seclusion. Her branch of the family were apparently not as well

off as the rest, because of a profligate father, and
Izzy had worked several jobs before trying her hand
at writing. "But poor Izzy never seemed to have
much money," the cousin commented, "no matter
how hard she worked. We're all ever so happy for
her now, even though it's a shame she seems to have
forgotten her dear family, who stood by her in her
time of greatest need."

That was pretty much it. Nothing else in the
folder hinted at anything in the least scandalous in
Isabella's personal life. I set it aside, disappointed,
though I had to chuckle over the cattiness of that
last remark. Once fame and fortune had come her
way, poor "Izzy" had no doubt found herself be-
sieged by cousins who hadn't given her the time of
day beforehand.

As novelists are wont to do, I indulged in a series
of what-ifs with regard to Isabella's life. What if,
during the war, she and her handsome flier had
anticipated their wedding vows and had their honey-
moon first? During wartime, even a girl raised as
conventionally as Isabella might do such a thing.
After all, they never knew when they might be together again.

I took it further. What if, after the handsome
flier's death, Isabella had suddenly found herself
pregnant, without benefit of that little band of
gold on the appropriate finger? What would a girl
from that kind of family do?

Go into seclusion for a year, have the baby in secret, then give it up for adoption: that's what she'd
do. What any "good girl" would have done back in
the forties if she had found herself in that situation.

Adoption! I picked up the folder, opened it, and
stared at the page containing Isabella's biography.

I looked at the list of awards. Isabella had been something of a patron to adoption agencies in Britain and had received a number of awards for her services to the same. Moreover, she had been made a dame not only for her distinguished contribution to British literature but also for her services to child welfare and adoption programs.

Bingo! I smiled, sure I had found the answer, though I had to admit that the evidence was all circumstantial, if not wholly the product of my own imagination.

Take it easy! I cautioned myself. So what if Isabella had borne a child out of wedlock back in the forties? Would she now be willing to kill someone to keep that fact hidden, after all this time? That child, if indeed there were one, would now be fifty-something.

The question was, how could I prove—or disprove—my little fantasy? There wasn't time to try to track down records. If I wanted results, I'd have to go straight to the source: Isabella herself. I spared a brief thought for my fledgling friendship with a writer I admired tremendously. What I planned to do would probably scotch any hopes of contact after this nasty little situation came to an end.

I could, of course, wait and let the police do their jobs. No doubt there was some kind of trace evidence that the folk in the lab could isolate to help prove the identity of the killer, but I'm just too nosy to sit by and wait. I wanted to be in the thick of things, and since the murderer would have a hard time putting me out of action (except with a big dose of garlic, the traditional wooden stake, or a silver bullet), I decided the risk of injury was minimal. The old bash on the head wouldn't do a thing to me.

Reaching for pen and paper, I began composing a note to Isabella. I'd leave a note under her door and wait to see the reaction. If she bit, I'd know that I was on to the truth. If she ignored the note, well, I might still be on to the truth, but I'd know that Isabella could play poker damn well.

Here's what I wrote:

> *My dear Isabella,*
>
> *If I may be of any assistance, please don't hesitate to ask. The sins of the past should remain just that; why should the events of five decades ago be made public now? Your work, both literary and charitable, is what really counts.*
>
> *Yours truly, etc., etc.*

To make sure she wouldn't miss the point, I underlined the word *charitable* twice.

Sealing the envelope, I sat and regarded it for a moment. I would have to let the police on duty see me deliver it, and I had no doubt that they would report my actions to Robin. But by the time he could question me about it, perhaps I'd have the results of my little ploy and would know whether my information would be of any use to him.

I opened my bedroom door and peered out. The two police officers were conferring at the other end of the hall and didn't seem to be paying much attention to this end. I moved quickly across the hall toward Isabella's door and dropped the note on the floor. With a smooth thrust of the foot, I got it under her door, then nipped back to my room. One of the officers whirled around just as I was going back into my room. I shut the door and waited right inside, listening. There was no sound of approaching footsteps, and I figured the two had gone back to their conversation, dismissing my little sortie from their concerns. So much the better!

To occupy myself while I awaited a response from Isabella, I picked up another of Giles's folders. Opening it, I read a brief biography of Lady Hermione Kinsale, countess of Mumsley. She was the only surviving child and heir to the seventh earl of Mumsley, Cholmondley Everard St. George Percival Kinsale. Percy had died in a hunting accident forty years ago, leaving young Hermione heiress to a large fortune, even after the ruinous death duties, which had crippled many aristocratic families over the past century.

Hermione had proved to have quite the head for business, for she had added considerably to the Kinsale coffers, and she had also been quite generous over the years with her wealth. She had endowed several scholarships for young women at various Oxbridge colleges, and she, like her friend Isabella Veryan, was noted as a friend to the cause of adoption and child welfare in Britain.

I paused at that. Quite an interesting link between the two women. Where had they first met? I wondered.

My speculations ended abruptly as my bedroom door flew open with a loud bang. I looked up to see Isabella Veryan advancing rapidly toward me, her eyes ablaze with fury, my note clutched in her right hand.

Stopping in front of me, she crumpled the note and threw it right into my face.

Chapter Twenty-two

The crumpled paper hit me between the eyes, and I drew back in my chair.

"Despicable! Utterly despicable!" Isabella spat the words out at me. "How I misjudged you! To think that you could resort to such a low trick."

"My dear Isabella," I said, getting to my feet, "please, calm yourself." I extended a hand, but she brushed it away and took a step backward.

"I thought you were a gentleman, Simon," Isabella said, her tone calmer, but the sudden pain in her eyes revealed her turmoil.

"My dear Isabella," I said again, my voice gentle, "please, do sit down." I gestured toward a chair, and, her shoulders slumping in exhaustion, Isabella sat down none too gracefully.

"I regret that you seem to have misunderstood the import of my note," I said, watching her closely and feeling more than a bit like a heel.

She would have none of that. "Come off it, Simon," she said. "You're trying to horn in on Nina's little blackmail game; that much is obvious." Tears began to trickle slowly down her face.

"You mistake me, Isabella," I said. "I have no intention of blackmailing you, I assure you." *Manipulate you, yes,* I thought, *but not blackmail you.* My one dead grandmother, a southern lady to the core, was no doubt spinning in her grave at my less than gentlemanly behavior at the moment, but I had never liked this particular grandmother anyway. Let her spin.

"I suppose you thought you were being so very clever, the way you worded your threatening little missive," Isabella said. She wiped away the tears with the back of one hand. "Nothing there that would appear out of the ordinary to anyone else."

"Again, I assure you, I have no intention of blackmailing you," I said, feeling like a parrot. "I want no part of whatever little game Nina is playing. I simply want to end it, once and for all, for the sake of all of us."

Her eyes narrowed in disbelief, Isabella regarded me. "Perhaps you don't know as much as I thought you might."

Nothing ventured, and all that. "Would it really matter to your readers, Isabella, that many years ago you had an illegitimate child and gave it up for adoption?"

She shrank back as if I had struck her. As, perhaps, I had. A trembling hand came up to her mouth as all color drained from her face.

"You do know," she whispered.

I felt no sense of triumph at my victory. I had reasoned correctly, but I had gambled.

Isabella drew a deep breath to steady herself. "What do you plan to do now with your knowledge, Simon?"

"I'm certainly not going to call up one of the tabloid papers and spill the story to them, if that's what you fear."

She relaxed a bit. "There must be something you want, however."

"The only thing I want is to get to the truth of what's going on here. Someone has killed twice and may kill again if we don't stop him or her."

"And you think *my* past has something to do with it?"

I shrugged. "Perhaps. Would you kill to keep the world from knowing that you had borne a child out of wedlock?"

"No!"

I waited.

"If I were to kill anyone," Isabella said in a softer tone, "it would be that bitch Nina."

"She found out about this somehow, didn't she?"

Isabella nodded.

"And she persuaded you, shall we say, to sign with her?"

Again Isabella nodded.

"Then what?" I asked.

"At first she was reasonable, once I got over the shock of such blatant blackmail. She wasn't very successful as an agent at that point, but once she had someone like me, with a recognizable name, there was no stopping her. I suppose the fact that her tactics had worked with me only served to encourage her."

"And so she found other candidates for her particular talents?"

"Unfortunately for them," Isabella said.

"So where did Wanda Harper fit in with all this?"

"I'm not quite certain, Simon," Isabella said. "I never met her until this weekend. But I think perhaps she might have worked for a private detective agency."

"Which is how Nina dug up the evidence she used in her little blackmail campaigns?"

"I believe so," Isabella said, shrugging. "But Nina has always been very careful not to reveal too much about how she came to know the things she does. By the time I discovered that someone had been digging into my past, it was too late to do anything about it."

"Other than give in to Nina's demands."

"Yes. At first she was reasonable, but the more successful I became, the more she wanted of me. She forced me increasingly into a more public role, which I deplored. For years I had lived quite happily and quietly, but the more exposure Nina got for me and my work, the less private my life became."

"Success demands a certain price," I said.

Isabella emitted a most unladylike snort at that. "I've had two stalkers, Simon, since I've become a best-selling author. Should I have to pay that kind of price? Being afraid to live alone in my own home? Having my heart leap into my throat every time the doorbell rings?"

"I had no idea, Isabella," I said, indignant for her sake. "I can see how intolerable that has been for you."

"Yes. My life has been anything but pleasant the past four years." She spoke the words without a trace of self-pity, and for that I had to admire her.

"Did you never think of simply publishing the

truth and thereby cutting Nina's feet from under her?"

"Publish and be damned, eh, Simon?" Her lips twisted in a grimace. "With the advantage of hindsight, I might have chosen to do so. But I might not." Her hands gripped the arms of her chair, and her knuckles whitened. "It would be like posing naked, exposing oneself in the most vulgar way. Having the rest of the world peer at you, jabbing at you without mercy, till you had no privacy left. Sometimes I think I'd rather die."

The horror in Isabella's voice was all too real, and I could understand the shame she would feel to have such intimate details of her life known to the public. Some *could* say, "Publish and be damned," and never think much about it, but for someone as intensely private as Isabella, such a course would be almost unthinkable.

She regarded me with eyes full of pain. "I simply don't have the courage, Simon. I didn't then, and I don't think I do now."

"I promise you, Isabella, that your secret is safe with me," I said. "As long as you had nothing to do with the murders, that is."

"I don't know of any way to convince you, Simon, that I didn't kill either of those wretched women. I found Norah tedious in the extreme, but I had no wish to see her die. Nor did I know the other woman well enough to wish her harm."

"Wanda Harper didn't attempt to blackmail you herself?"

"No, she didn't, though she did accost me yesterday on Nina's behalf. She may have done the research, but Nina usually reserved for herself the joy of watching us squirm, like butterflies impaled upon pins."

I grinned. "Now it's Nina's turn to squirm."

"If there is any justice to be had," Isabella said, the ghost of a smile hovering around her lips. She paused a moment before continuing. "You've said not a word, Simon, about my child."

What should I say now? I wondered. Since I had simply guessed that the child existed and knew nothing else whatsoever about him or her, I was caught by my own bluff.

Isabella read my indecision correctly. With a rueful smile she said, "You really didn't know for sure, did you? And I walked right into your little trap."

"Is the identity of your child important to what has happened here?"

She stood up. "No. Not in the least." She walked to the door before turning to face me again. "I believe Nina has met her match in you, Simon. You're every bit the manipulator she is. But perhaps your motives are less self-serving. At least, I'm hoping they are."

I sat in silence as she left the room, closing the door softly behind her. I felt a moment's regret that any friendship I might have had with Isabella Veryan had little chance of blossoming now. I had played a rather unpleasant trick on her, and she might never be able to forgive me for that. That pained me, for I admired both the woman and her work tremendously.

She had lied to me, however, and the consequences of that lie remained to be discerned.

When she denied that the identity of her child was of any relevance to the murders here at Kinsale House, she had lied. She didn't know I could read her that easily, and probably thought that had put an end to the issue. I had felt the quickening of her pulse as she uttered the denial, and I knew she had lied to me.

Could Isabella's son or daughter be among those present at Kinsale House?

Chapter Twenty-three

That was an interesting thought. Someone here at Kinsale House this week could be the illegitimate son or daughter of a best-selling mystery writer. What headlines that would make! Nina could certainly get lots of publicity out of that for Isabella, and no doubt her sales would climb even higher as a result.

Who could it be? One of the attendees, a wannabe writer? Possible, I thought, but not as interesting if it turned out to be one of the other writers.

Could it have been Norah Tattersall? But no, I decided; if it had been Norah, Isabella would surely have been more upset by her death. She had disliked Norah intensely, but if Norah had been her daughter, she wouldn't have been so unaffected by her death. Isabella was not that cold and unfeeling, I was sure.

I reached for the folders containing the results

of Giles's research. I first looked at the date of Isabella's birth. She was a bit older than I had thought, nearer eighty than seventy, though she certainly didn't look it. Her child would now be in his or her fifties, and there were two among us who fit in that age group: Dexter Harbaugh and Patty Anne Putney. I checked the biographical information about each of them, and their birth dates confirmed what I had reckoned. Harbaugh was fifty-six, and Putney was about nine months younger. So it could be either of them, based on their dates of birth.

I delved further into their bios. Nothing in the accounts of their lives suggested that they had been adopted. Dexter Harbaugh was the son of a vicar in Surrey, and Patty Anne Putney had grown up in Devon, the daughter of a farmer.

Since the biographies yielded nothing, I skimmed the various interviews that Giles had found with each of them. Again, nothing. Neither ever said anything about having been adopted. In fact, neither of them said much at all about their respective childhoods.

Frustrated for the moment, I put the folders aside and sat staring into space. What would it matter if either Dexter Harbaugh or Patty Anne Putney really was the biological offspring of Isabella Veryan? Isabella would be appalled to have the indiscretions of her youth exposed to the public, and she might prefer not to claim someone as unpleasant as Dexter Harbaugh or as potty as Patty Anne Putney as her child.

But was any of this a solid motive for murder? As Isabella had herself observed, if she were going to murder anyone, it would most likely be Nina Yaknova. Wanda Harper had been merely Nina's employee, and Norah Tattersall only a foolish witness, perhaps, to the first murder.

What had Wanda Harper done to make someone want to kill her? I had a better motive, in some ways, than anyone else, as far as I knew. Because Nina was behind Wanda's impersonation of me, though, Nina was a more likely target than Wanda, should I have chosen to solve the problem by murder.

There was something I was missing; that much was obvious. Something to do with Wanda Harper and her connections to my fellow guests at Kinsale House. What was it, and how could I uncover it?

Giles interrupted my futile musings, bursting into the room with a tipsy smile and a hearty "Hullo, Simon!"

I stood up as Giles nearly tripped and fell into my arms. "You've been drinking, Giles."

He grinned at me as he steadied himself with my assistance. "Quite right, Simon, I have. So would you have been. Absolutely ghastly dinner, I can tell you." He burped. "Food was horrible, but the company was worse. Appallingly common, they all are, as my dear mater would say." He burped again.

"I think you need to lie down for a bit, Giles." I had never seen him in this state before, and I wasn't amused.

He grinned and opened his mouth to speak, but I forestalled him. "And no, Giles, I will not lie down with you. Certainly not now, when you're three sheets to the wind."

"Only two, Simon, only two." He sat down on the edge of my bed.

"Even so, Giles, I think you need a nap more than you need anything else."

" 'S what you always say, Simon," he said. "Doesn't

matter. Lady Hermione wants you downstairs anyway."

"Right now?" I said. "Whatever for?"

"Didn't say," Giles said between burps. "Wants all the writers in the drawing room right away. Said I'd tell you." He sank back on the bed and was asleep a moment later.

I shook my head as I removed his shoes and turned him around so that his whole body was on the bed. I covered him with a blanket and left him to snore in peace while I went downstairs to discover what it was that Lady Hermione wanted.

Downstairs I found that good lady awaiting my arrival none too patiently.

"Sorry I'm late, Lady Hermione," I said, "but your message was somewhat delayed in the delivery."

"Yes, I could see young Blitherington might have trouble conveying it," Lady Hermione responded sourly, "but at least you're here. Please take a seat." She waved a hand at the company seated around where she stood.

To her left, Isabella Veryan and George Austen-Hare occupied one sofa, while Patty Anne Putney and Dexter Harbaugh sat in chairs on either side of them. Nina Yaknova and Ashford Dunn sat close together on the sofa to the right of Lady Hermione. There was an empty chair beside it, which I took, being none too pleased at having to sit near Nina and her best-selling hack. As I sat, I could see one of Robin Chase's men hovering discreetly in the background beyond Isabella and George.

"I have spoken with Detective Inspector Chase," Lady Hermione began, and for once her voice wasn't raising the rafters, "and he has informed me that we may proceed with our schedule of workshops."

"Really, Lady Hermione," Dexter Harbaugh said, "do you think that is wise? Given the circumstances?"

I watched him with interest, my eyes roving back and forth between his face and that of Isabella Veryan, hoping to spot some likeness of feature or gesture.

"Anyone who is afraid to remain in this house may leave tomorrow," Lady Hermione announced, though her tone made it clear how contemptible she would find anyone who admitted to such fear. "Detective Inspector Chase has given permission for that, of course. I would prefer you all to remain here and continue with the program as planned."

"Mr. Murbles is most unhappy, Hermione," Patty Anne Putney spoke, and I examined her with the same interest I had Dexter Harbaugh. For the moment, though, I could see nothing about either her or Harbaugh that reminded me of Isabella Veryan. "He is quite unused to being exposed to such an atmosphere of violence, and he would prefer to go home as soon as possible."

Ashford Dunn leaned into Nina and muttered something into her ear.

"What did you say, Mr. Dunn?" Lady Hermione spoke in such a firm tone that Dunn jerked back, startled.

He looked at Lady Hermione like a schoolboy being admonished by his teacher.

"Speak up, Mr. Dunn," Lady Hermione said when he simply mumbled at her.

"I said, 'Why can't she speak for herself, instead of always pretending that stuffed rabbit is talking?'" Dunn replied. "Absolutely potty, she is, always going on about 'the rabbit says this' and 'the rabbit says that.'"

His words trailed off into a strained silence as he

realized that several pairs of eyes were regarding him with utter loathing.

Isabella Veryan was the first to speak. "Thank you, Mr. Dunn, for confirming what the rest of us have suspected. You are every bit as unintelligent and unfeeling as we thought from having read what little we could stomach of your so-called novels." She reached out a hand to comfort the now sniffling Patty Anne Putney, who clasped her hand gratefully. Mr. Murbles, however, seemed not in the least affected by Dunn's gross insensitivity.

I could feel Dunn wanting desperately to be able to shrivel up and disappear into the sofa. His attempted brashness was no match for Isabella's cutting aristocratic contempt.

Nina was made of sterner stuff than Dunn. "Dear Isabella to the rescue of the poor, defenseless child," she said. She held Isabella's gaze, challenging her, but Isabella never wavered. "So *maternal* of you, Isabella. It's a pity you never had children, I must say."

Isabella looked away from Nina for a moment, her eyes seeking mine. I nodded, once, and Isabella drew a deep breath, steeling herself. Nina had been waiting, smiling, to see how Isabella would respond to her bait.

"I think the time has come, Nina, to end this once and for all. I'm so weary of you and your pitiful lack of ethics or any moral sense whatsoever that I'd rather face any scandal that might result."

The withering contempt in Isabella's voice got to Nina, I could tell. Nina was so used to having others cower before her that she didn't quite know how to handle someone who stood up to her as magnificently as Isabella was doing. She groped for something to say in the face of Isabella's words but failed.

"You have talent, Nina," Isabella continued. "I'll grant you that. But it's a pity that you couldn't rely on your talent to bring you success. You have the insight and the energy to be a successful agent, but you have no moral center. Instead, you use the most vile and contemptible methods to get what you want, and you don't care how it affects anyone else."

I wanted to clap to encourage Isabella, because I was enjoying this mightily. Nina might never squirm this much again, and she deserved every unpleasant second of it. Probably for the first time in her career as an agent, she was utterly speechless.

The others stared at Isabella in fascination, wondering what was coming. All except Lady Hermione, that is; she watched her old friend with eyes full of sympathy and a shared pain at what this was costing Isabella.

"As Nina well knows," Isabella said, her voice tight and controlled, "I do have a child, though that child has no idea I am his mother."

Then it's Dexter Harbaugh, I thought. *No wonder Isabella didn't want him to know, the prat.*

"It's an old story, one you've all read many times before, in many books. It's the story of a young woman in love with a charming man, who anticipates her wedding vows, then finds herself in trouble and the man nowhere around to help her face the consequences." She laughed, a bitter, painful sound. "In my case, at least, it wasn't because the man knew and didn't want to help. He was killed in the war before he ever knew he was going to be a father."

Isabella paused, and everyone in the room waited, hardly daring to breathe, for her to continue. The policeman was so fascinated that he had forgotten the notebook and pencil clasped in his hands.

"I never wanted you to find out this way," Isabella said, staring down at her hands, clasped together in her lap. At this point, she was speaking to only one person in the room. "Dear George, do forgive me, but I'm your mother."

Chapter Twenty-four

I was just as stunned as nearly everyone else in the room by Isabella's revelation.

George Austen-Hare was her son? I had never even considered him, because I had thought he was in his sixties and thus too old. I regarded him with fresh eyes, and now I could see that he was younger than I had thought.

As the moment of shock passed, I looked around to note everyone else's reactions. Nina was angry to have her bluff called; Isabella had effectively spiked her guns. Lady Hermione had likely been privy to the truth for many years.

One other person did not appear surprised at the revelation, however, and that was another surprise. George Austen-Hare had not reacted as one might have expected him to when faced with such an admission.

George sat quietly smiling at Isabella, waiting

for the shock of his mother's announcement to wear off before he spoke.

"No need to apologize, Isabella," he said. "I've known for quite some time, so it's not news to me."

"But, George," Isabella said, trying to gain control of her voice, "you never let on. You've never said a word, even hinted."

George tilted his head to one side and shrugged. "Didn't really bother me that much, to be honest. I had already got to know you a bit when I found out, and I understood your point of view."

"Oh, George, my dear boy," Isabella said, tears streaming down her cheeks as she clasped one of George's hands in hers.

"My parents told me a bit about you when I was a big enough lad to understand. Never told me your name, of course, but we talked about it and why you had had to give me up for adoption. Wonderful people, my parents." He beamed at us, apparently not in the least disconcerted by talking about something so personal.

"Isn't this just too terribly sweet?" Nina had at last found her voice. "What a lovely little reunion! And think what a field day the tabloids will have with this story. The best-selling mystery writer whose bastard turns out to be a mystery writer, too."

Not even I could have anticipated what happened next. Lady Hermione moved so quickly, it happened before any of us could do anything to prevent it, even if we had wanted to. The sound of her hand connecting with Nina's cheek reverberated through the room.

"*Bravissima,* Lady Hermione, *bravissima!*" Dexter Harbaugh crowed with laughter as he stood and applauded what our hostess had done.

Her face reddening with the imprint of Lady

Hermione's hand, Nina sputtered furiously, "You bloody cow! I'll have you brought up on charges for assault. How dare you!"

"Go right ahead, you common little piece of gutter trash," Lady Hermione said, her eyes glittering in triumph. "I've been itching to do that for years, and by God, it was worth it."

Nina fought to regain control of her emotions, and no one spoke for a moment. Then Nina had her revenge. "Perhaps you'll come to regret it, *Lady* Hermione, when everyone sees the pictures I have of the little trysts you've been having in a hotel in Lyme Regis with your butler. You'll be a laughing-stock, you raddled old bitch!"

Oh, my! Try as I might, I couldn't quite grasp the thought of Lady Hermione making the beast with two backs with Dingleby. Dingleby? This was getting more ridiculous by the minute.

Nearly everyone's jaw had dropped at that little bit of news, I noticed as I looked around the room. Only Isabella seemed to have known about this little peccadillo of her dear friend.

Lady Hermione had paled at Nina's attack, but she was a game old girl. "Perhaps, Nina," Lady Hermione said, her voice admirably cool, "but I'll still be the countess of Kinsale. You, however, will never be anything but unbearably common."

With more dignity than I ever supposed she could muster, Nina got to her feet. "I suppose I am common, Lady Hermione," she said. "I've had to fight for everything I ever wanted. I didn't get a stately home and a fortune handed to me at birth. But you couldn't care less about that." She paused, surveying us each briefly in turn. "I won't forget a single word that any of you has said to me. Remember that."

The cold hatred in her voice boded ill for all of us. Nina wanted revenge for her humiliation. How could we thwart her? Other than killing her, that is.

"I wouldn't do anything too rash if I were you, Nina," I said. "Have you stopped to think what would happen to your career as an agent if it became known just how you get your authors to sign with you?"

"He's right, Nina," Isabella said. "You can't blackmail your way out of this one."

"I can certainly see to it that all of you are exposed for what you really are," Nina said, still defiant, though her words lacked conviction.

"Yes, Nina, you can expose all our little secrets to the public if you like," George Austen-Hare said, his mother's hand still clasped in his own. "You could very well make all of us laughingstocks in the public eye. You would also be exposing your own role in all of it, too. How many publishers or authors do you think would have anything to do with you after that?"

That stopped Nina cold. She hadn't taken time to think it completely through, but as she stood there, comprehension began to dawn. George was right. The risk of exposure was too great; she would take herself down with the rest of us.

"Very well," Nina said. "You've won this round. But if any of you get in my way ever again, I'll make you pay, no matter what it might cost me."

What an exit line! Bette Davis couldn't have done it any better. We watched as Nina stalked from the room, relieved to see her go, but at the same time a bit unsure of what she might yet do.

"Aren't you going with her?" Dexter Harbaugh addressed Ashford Dunn pugnaciously, coming over to stand over the younger man where he still sat on the sofa.

"I think I'll let her cool off first," Dunn said, grinning up at Dexter.

"You know what they say about playing with fire, young man," Lady Hermione said.

Dunn just kept grinning. "I won't get burned; you can count on that."

"Oh, really," Isabella said. "I suppose you expect us all to believe that you're different from the rest of us, that you signed with Nina of your own free will?"

"Can I help it if I've led a blameless life, unlike the rest of you?" Dunn said. He sniggered.

"Nonsense!" Lady Hermione snorted in derision to punctuate that one word. "Don't trust that viper. Sooner or later, you'll come to regret it. Because whatever she knows about you, she'll use. She doesn't know any other way to operate."

Dunn stood up. "Thanks for the advice, lady. But I'm going to make Nina so much money, she'll be doing what I say; trust me on that."

I had to admire his performance. He was putting up a good front for the benefit of everyone in the room, including himself. He may have persuaded the others with his air of absolute confidence, but I could sense the uncertainty beneath. Dunn had something to hide, just like the rest of us. What was it?

"Now, if you will excuse me," Dunn said, "I think I will go and have a little conference with my agent now."

No one responded as Dunn walked out of the room. The policeman, who had long been forgotten by the rest of the group, approached the door moments after Dunn had closed it. He stepped out into the hall, and I could hear him having a whispered conversation with someone outside the door, though I couldn't make out the words. No doubt he was passing along the gist of what had transpired in this room. Robin Chase would soon be apprised of these latest developments. What would he make of it all?

Lady Hermione claimed my attention by clearing her throat. "On to business," she said. She meant what she said. She told us exactly what she expected of us over the remaining time at Kinsale House. I thought she was being overly optimistic that the conference attendees would want to stay on at Kinsale House after tomorrow, when, Robin Chase had said, anyone who wished to do so might leave. But human nature being what it is, perhaps enough of the attendees would linger to make the continued presence of the writers necessary. I was certainly willing to remain, and so, it appeared, were the others.

Robin Chase appeared at that point with an announcement that got a frosty reception. "My apologies, ladies and gentlemen. I do realize the hour is late, but I'm afraid that I need to speak again with each of you in turn." He held up a hand to stop the burgeoning protests. "I can assure you that I will conduct the interviews as quickly as possible. I know you must all be exhausted from the events of the day, but I'm afraid I must insist."

"Very well, Detective Inspector," Lady Hermione said, speaking for all of us. "We must do our duty." She rose to accompany him.

"I beg your pardon, Lady Hermione," Robin said, "but if I might, I'd like to speak first with Dr. Kirby-Jones."

Frowning in annoyance, Lady Hermione sank back down into her chair. Nodding first in her direction, then offering the others a polite wave, I followed Robin from the room.

Robin waited until I had settled into my chair before beginning. "Tell me, Simon, what happened in that room. I want to hear your take on it."

I repeated it all, as best I could, to Robin. He nodded occasionally as his eyes wandered back and forth between me and several pages of notes spread before him on the desk.

"Thank you, Simon," he said. "That tallies with what the PC took down." He rubbed a hand across his face. "Looks like Miss Yaknova was running quite a little blackmail racket. So, tell me, Simon, what was she blackmailing you over?"

I had to laugh. "Not a thing, Robin, not a thing." You'll note that I didn't say I had nothing to hide. I had to hope that Nina would never uncover the one secret that I intended to keep well and truly hidden from her.

"Then why were you immune? What is different with you?"

Either Robin was being deliberately dense, or he wasn't as sharp as I thought him to be. "She wasn't blackmailing me, but surely you can see how she was trying to manipulate me."

"Because she had her associate posing as 'Dorinda Darlington,' you mean."

"Exactly," I said, pleased that he had got it after all.

"What could she hope to gain from that, Simon?"

"In a word, publicity." I shrugged. "Nina had been trying to get me to let her leak the news that I am Dorinda Darlington. She thought the resulting publicity would give my sales a big boost, despite the fact that I'm doing quite well as it is. I refused, and I think she must have come up with this scheme to try to force me into it."

"Very sneaky, and ethically questionable."

"To say the least."

Robin made a tent of his fingers and flexed them repeatedly. "But her scheme misfired rather badly when someone murdered her associate."

"And it wasn't I who did that, I can assure you, Robin. Nor was it Giles."

"I know, Simon. Neither you nor Sir Giles is a murderer." He frowned at me, trying to appear disapproving. "But you have both been scurrying around behind the scenes, trying to interfere in my investigation."

"I beg to differ with you, Robin. Neither Giles nor I would ever want to interfere with your investigation." I smiled my most charming smile. "Merely assist, never interfere."

"You may assist me more effectively by *not* assisting, I assure you, except when I require information from you." Robin's tone was repressive, but I thought I detected a twinkle in his eye. "Let us clarify a few things, in case you have come across something that my men and I might have missed."

"Certainly." I was nothing if not cooperative.

"Dame Isabella Veryan was anxious to keep hidden the fact that she had borne a child out of wedlock more than fifty years ago. Moreover, that her child was none other than her fellow mystery writer George Austen-Hare. Mr. Austen-Hare, for his part, was not keen on having it known that he'd had an affair with the first murder victim. An affair, moreover, that was engineered on her part in order to make him go along with Miss Yaknova's schemes."

"Good for George," I said approvingly. "I told him it would be better for him if he came to you himself."

"He did," Robin acknowledged. "Though he was unaware at the time that we had already come into possession of certain photographs Ms. Harper had in her room. Photographs that made the nature of their association all too clear."

"Oh, dear," I said. "Poor old George."

"To continue," Robin said. "Dexter Harbaugh is deathly afraid of the dark and of spiders. Neither fact which he would want his reading public to know, because it would tarnish his credibility as a writer of extremely hard-boiled crime fiction."

Robin did his best not to laugh, and I had to look away from him to keep from bursting out with a chuckle or two myself.

"Lady Hermione Kinsale has been having a torrid and none too discreet affair with her butler, Dingleby, who is some thirty years or so her junior." Again, Robin was doing his best not to react.

"That's it so far," I said.

"And that's all we've got so far," Robin said, sighing tiredly. "Patty Anne Putney just seems plain barmy, but I don't know that that would come as a great surprise to her readers. Nor that it would matter all that much."

"Probably not," I said. "Though she seems more than a bit unstable, if you ask me. What if someone threatened her rabbit? She's already reacted violently once, when Nina tore the silly thing's head off."

Robin grimaced. "After that happened, we did a

little checking. It seems Miss Putney has a history of such little incidents. She has attacked several people in the past, for very much the same reason."

I stared at Robin. Could the answer to the two murders be that simple after all?

Chapter Twenty-five

———— ☠ ————

"I've already considered that, Simon," Robin said, reading my mind rather easily for once. "Of all the suspects, Miss Putney is the only one who has any recorded history of violent acts toward others. When I discovered that, I must admit she became my favorite choice for the murderer."

"But . . ." I said, as he paused.

"However," Robin continued with a small smile, "Miss Putney has a reasonably good alibi for one of the two murders."

"And you don't think there are two murderers at work here?"

"No, I don't." Robin was very firm.

"Then Potty Patty can't be our murderer."

"Er, no, Simon, she can't." Robin gave me his most professional look, not deigning to comment on the sobriquet I had bestowed. "She was in the presence of several of the attendees during the time in question, and she never left the room."

Gazing with fascination at my own hands, I said, "I do realize, Robin, that you have shown extraordinary trust thus far in discussing these matters with me as you have. If I might impose upon that trust a bit further, might I ask if you have any idea who the murderer is?" I glanced up then to see how he was taking my efforts at diplomacy.

Robin gazed at me through narrowed eyelids. I wondered fleetingly what he would have said, had not one of his subordinates been present. "I am not at liberty to say at the moment, Simon, though I assure you my men and I have things well in hand."

Why did he clam up all of a sudden? Perhaps he had no idea who the killer was, or perhaps he did and was simply waiting to find the evidence he needed to proceed with an arrest. Either way, I realized that he had nothing more to say to me at that point.

Robin stood. "Thank you, Simon, as always, for your very willing assistance in our inquiries."

"And as always, you are most welcome, Robin." I grinned, then turned and walked out of the room.

On the way up to my bedroom, I continued to speculate. Did Robin know, or didn't he? I hated not knowing. I had narrowed the field down in my own mind to two suspects, but I still didn't know why. And frankly, I was just too damn nosy to wait to hear it from Robin. I wanted to know, and I wanted to know as soon as possible.

All of which meant, naturally, that I would have to take matters into my own hands. Be a catalyst, as it were. If I didn't, there was no telling how long this dreary affair might drag on, and I was ready to be done with Kinsale House. I would, of course, fulfill my obligation to Lady Hermione, however she saw fit.

Giles continued to snore in peace on my bed, and I sat for a few minutes watching him as I thought about what I wanted to do and how best to achieve it. Robin would no doubt be rather angry with me, particularly if I was wrong and the whole thing somehow misfired. But he would get over it, one way or another. And if I was right, well, then Robin would be welcome to take all the credit. I wasn't seeking the limelight—at least, not in this way.

The thought of danger didn't bother me, because only a few things could really harm me permanently. Since I very much doubted that anyone at Kinsale House knew I was a vampire, I reckoned I should be safe.

The tricky part would be working around the men that Robin had stationed in the house, not letting them know what was going on until I actually needed them to collar the murderer. After, that is, I had wrung the confession out of him or her. Unlike vampires of old, I can't shape-change, or turn myself into a mist and slip under someone's door, then reassemble all the molecules and all that rot. I'm thoroughly corporeal these days, though I have to admit that sometimes it might be quite a lark to go misting about.

Giles had had enough of a nap by now to sleep off the worst effects of his excess of drink at dinner. Time to wake him up, which I did, more gently than he deserved.

"What is it, Simon? What do you want?" Giles regarded me with bleary eyes as he tried to focus.

"I want you to wake up, Giles. I need your help with something." I sat beside him on the bed and poked him in the side.

Giles stretched one arm above his head for a moment and yawned, then leaned in toward me and rested his hand on my thigh. "I'm ready, Simon. How may I be of assistance?"

"If you don't behave, Giles," I said in a severe tone, "I shall pour cold water over your head." I got up from the bed and stood beside it, staring down at him.

Giles yawned as he sat up. "Very well. Pardon me, but I'm knackered. What is it you want then, Simon? More bloody boring research?"

"If you're awake and listening now, Giles, I shall tell you." I sat down in my chair, and Giles folded his legs under him and sat in a semi-lotus position on the bed.

"I'm listening."

I gave him a quick summary of everything that had occurred downstairs, and soon his eyes were wide open with interest. I concluded with my interview with Robin.

"What are you going to do now, Simon? Surely you're not going to sit by patiently and wait for Robin, are you?" His cheeky grin was all too knowing.

"No, Giles, I'm not. The first thing I'm going to do is a little reading. The research you've done, which you've called boring, has actually been tremendously useful. I suspect it may yield more helpful information in one particular case. And I want you to be ready to help me in case I need to dig up something else."

Giles saluted smartly. *"Ja wohl, Herr Commandant!"*

"Leave the humor aside, Giles, and go splash some water on your face."

Muttering under his breath, Giles did as I asked. I turned to the stack of folders Giles had put together, and searched through them for a particular one. Opening it, I began skimming through what Giles had been able to unearth on Ashford Dunn. I didn't believe he had lived a blameless life, as he had so cheekily asserted earlier, and I was convinced there had to be something in his past that had made him vulnerable to Nina and her methods.

Giles hadn't been able to find much about Dunn. Before now he hadn't granted many interviews, and the media mentions Giles had unearthed were all items about him that revealed only the broadest details of his life. Born and reared in Iowa, he had attended the state university there, then had gone on to law school in the East. His school was not one of the better-known ones, but he had clerked at the Iowa State Supreme Court, and afterward he had landed a job at a prestigious firm. Then, suddenly, two years ago, after only two years at the firm, he had quit his job to devote himself to writing.

I sat and thought about that résumé for a moment. Dunn hadn't had a particularly distinguished academic career, yet he had apparently had a brilliant, albeit brief, career as a lawyer. Something about that combination didn't ring true.

"Giles!" I called to Giles, who was in his room fiddling about with his laptop.

He came to the door. "Yes, Simon?"

"Here's what I want you to do." I glanced at my watch. It was still only a few minutes before nine.

"There's still time to call the States before offices close down for the evening. I want you to make a few phone calls for me and see what you can find out about Ashford Dunn." Quickly I sketched out what I wanted to know, and how I thought Giles might obtain the information.

Giles grinned. "What fun, Simon! I can look up the phone numbers on the Internet, and the rest I can talk my way through."

"Good! Go to it." I sat back and waited and let him do his own particular brand of magic. I could have made the calls myself, of course, after having Giles obtain the proper phone numbers for me. But Giles has considerable charm, not to mention a voice and an accent that can talk most people into doing any number of things they wouldn't normally do. (It's a good thing for both our sakes that I'm not most people.)

In less than half an hour, Giles had found out what I wanted to know. It's amazing how willing some people are to talk, even when they shouldn't. The urge to gossip is very basic to human nature, luckily for nosy folk like me!

Giles laughed gleefully as he recounted what he had learned from one of the secretaries at the law school. "Lucky for us, Simon, that I hit upon a dear old thing who had been at the law school for donkey's years. She couldn't tell me what you wanted to know fast enough."

"Did Dunn actually attend law school there?"

"Yes, he did," Giles replied. "He made it through three semesters by the skin of his teeth, according to our dear, helpful Mrs. Mills from Iowa. If he hadn't been so good-looking and able to talk himself out of various scrapes, he would have 'flunked out'—I believe that was the phrase she used."

"Quite a helpful lady," I observed.

"She would have been even more helpful had I had the time to indulge her." Giles laughed. "I also asked her whether she knew anyone named Wanda Harper, and you were right about that one, too. Seems Harper worked there briefly at the law school, and it was at the same time that Dunn was a student. The old girl had lots more stories to tell, but those were the main things you wanted to know. But there is one other and very important fact."

"Which is?"

"According to Mrs. Mills, Dunn never graduated from that law school. He was supposed to be transferring to another school, but she said she very much doubted another school would have taken him."

"Ah! Very interesting! If he had transferred to another school, he would have said in his bio." I frowned. "That certainly makes a clerkship at the state supreme court unlikely."

"Exactly," Giles said. "Now, on to the next call. I was able to talk to someone in the personnel office at the law firm where Dunn said he worked for a couple of years." His grin grew even broader.

"Okay, give! What did you find out?"

Giles flashed me a big smile. "They never heard of him. I asked how he could go around claiming to have been an employee of theirs, and the chap said that the firm employs several hundred lawyers in offices around the world. Unless someone bothered to check, it might not come to their attention that someone claimed to have worked there. But he assured me that Dunn had never been employed by this firm."

"So Ashford Dunn's legal background is very shaky, to say the least. He's not a bona fide lawyer."

"Doesn't sound like it to me, Simon."

"He's a fake, Giles, and he knew the first victim before he ever came to England. Add that all together, and we have an excellent motive for murder."

Chapter Twenty-six

"Time to put the next part of the plan into motion, Giles," I said. Quickly I outlined what I wanted him to do. "Got it?"

"Got it, Simon. You can count on me." His earnest smile reassured me. "I'll be waiting right here with my mobile phone."

I tapped my pocket. "And mine is here, ready to ring with the signal should I need you." I walked over and picked up the phone from the bedside table. I punched in the butler's extension and waited.

"Ah, Dingleby, could you tell me how I might find Miss Yaknova's room?"

Dingleby could and did. I thanked him and rang off. "Here I go, Giles," I said. "Wish me luck."

"How about a kiss for luck, Simon?" His saucy stare offered an invitation that I decided not to resist, just this once. I leaned toward him and brushed his lips with mine.

I drew back to find him pouting. "Always leave them wanting more, eh, Simon?" he said.

"Exactly! Now, don't fall asleep!"

"I won't," Giles said. "Be on your way."

In the hall, the door closed behind me, I stood for a moment and eyed the guards Robin had posted in the hallway. As long as I acted as though I weren't doing anything wrong, perhaps they wouldn't stop me. According to Dingleby, Nina's room was on this same floor, down the other wing. Ashford Dunn occupied the room next to her. I headed in that direction, nodding politely to the guard posted near the head of the stairs. He returned my nod and let me pass without question.

I counted the doors until I got to the right one. I knocked, and a moment later I heard Nina's voice. "Who is it, and what do you want?"

"It's Simon, Nina, and I want to talk to you."

I waited a moment; then the door opened. Nina glared at me. "What the hell do you want, Simon?"

"If I might come in, Nina, I have a little proposition for you."

She stared at me for a moment, considering. Then, stepping back, she opened the door and motioned for me to enter.

I did my best to ignore the so-called decor of this room. It was just as spacious and just as hideous as my own. Unlike mine, however, it reeked of cigarette smoke. Lady Hermione would not be pleased at having to air this room out for a week or two, but I doubted Nina cared that much how Lady Hermione would react.

The door that connected this room to the next one was closed at the moment, but I figured that

Ashford Dunn was there, with his ear to the keyhole, figuratively if not literally. He'd be well aware of what transpired in this room, which was just what I wanted.

Nina lighted another cigarette before motioning for me to sit. I sat down and waited for her to take a seat near me. The chairs were only a few feet from the connecting door, which suited my little scheme perfectly.

"What is this little proposition of yours, Simon?"

I had waited for Nina to speak first. Normally, she would have waited me out, but perhaps she was tired of playing her usual little games.

"I believe you will agree, Nina, that we all now find ourselves in a rather difficult, not to say delicate, position with the events of the last day or so." I was giving it my pompous best, and I could see Nina's eyebrows beginning to twitch in irritation. "You find yourself suddenly without some of your most stellar clients, not to mention that they're also some of your biggest earners. We, on the other hand, find ourselves needing an agent who will be as aggressive as you have been in making good deals for us. It seems to me, therefore, that we each need something, and perhaps we can come to some kind of accommodation."

"Your point being . . . ?" Nina said, expelling smoke in a furious puff. "Stop gas-bagging it, Simon. Did the others appoint you their spokesman?"

"No, Nina, I'm speaking on my own behalf. The others may choose to do the same thing, of course. But this is about me." I paused to let her think about that for a moment. "I need something from you, but I think perhaps you need more from me."

Nina's eyebrows rose at that. "Go on."

"Here it is. I'm willing to let you continue as my

agent, but we have to agree on certain terms. You will not—I repeat, *not*—come up with any more little schemes to force me into going public about my books. Is that understood?"

I got a very expressive rolling of the eyes for that one. She sat and thought for a moment. "Understood, Simon. What else?"

"You will sign a statement to that effect, to be witnessed by my solicitor, and kept on file in their offices."

"Oh, really, Simon. That's a bit much, don't you think?"

"No, Nina, I don't think. Someone needs to hang tough on you, and it might as well be me."

"Very well, then. I will sign a statement to that effect."

"Good," I said, offering her a smile. "Then I think we can do business."

"Is that it?"

"Not quite," I said. I sat and waited for a moment. "You're also going to have to give up the boy toy next door."

"What do you mean, Simon? Don't be absurd. Why should I give up Ash? He's going to make us both millions!" Nina ground out her cigarette in an ashtray already overflowing with butts and immediately reached for another.

"Do you really want to be in bed with a murderer, Nina?" I asked in an intentionally offensive tone.

"Surely you're not saying that Ash murdered those two women?" Nina's outrage might have convinced someone else, but it didn't convince me.

"Come off it, Nina. Either he did it or you did. Nothing else makes sense."

She didn't respond.

"Well, Nina, dearest, did *you* kill them?"

"No, I did not!" she snapped back at me.

"There you are, then. Ashford Dunn killed them."

"Why would he do that?" Enough scorn dripped from those words to make a good-sized puddle on the hideous carpet.

"Because, my dear Nina, he's an absolute fake, and you know it." I listened closely, and I could hear the knob turning, oh, so quietly, on the connecting door. Dunn was definitely listening to what was going on in here.

"A fake? How so?"

Nina wasn't going to give an inch; that was clear. "Don't be bloody stupid, Nina. The game is up, and it's time you realized it. If you're not careful, you're going to end up in prison with him. Is that what you want?"

She remained obdurate. She just sat there and stared at me.

"Look, Nina, I know he's not really a lawyer, and it won't be long before Robin Chase knows it, too. How is it going to look to his publishers, who've laid out quite a lot of money, when Dunn is exposed in all the tabloids as someone who couldn't manage to finish law school? Nor did he clerk at the Iowa Supreme Court or have a job with a prestigious law firm in Boston. He's a fake, pure and simple, and he killed two women to cover that up."

Still Nina said nothing.

"If that's not enough for you, my dear, how about this? Were you aware that Dunn and Wanda Harper knew each other back in Iowa? When he was a student—and evidently not a very good one— and she worked in the law school's office?"

That one really rankled her, even though she wasn't saying anything yet.

"And one more thing, dearest Nina. I'll bet it was Wanda Harper who introduced you to our young Mr. Dunn. Wasn't it?" I didn't wait for an acknowledgment. "They reeled you right in, had you right where they wanted you."

Nina cut loose with a string of profanities, many of which focused on the murderous Mr. Dunn and his less-than-illustrious forebears. Lady Hermione would no doubt have found it exceedingly common. I was simply relieved to have gotten through to her at last. After this, Nina would be willing to shop her boy toy, no question.

"I take it, then, you're ready to see sense, Nina, dear?"

"That bloody wanker!" Nina said, the flow of obscenities having weakened into the merest trickle. "I can't believe him—or that bitch Wanda. They set me up. They bloody well set me up!"

"So you'll be more than happy to cooperate with the police?"

"I can't get to that dishy detective fast enough, Simon," Nina assured me. "I'll nail that wanker's balls to the wall; see if I don't."

Poor Nina had been aching to rip someone to shreds, ever since Lady Hermione had humiliated her downstairs. Dunn deserved everything that was coming to him, and he'd be lucky if Robin got to him before Nina did.

I was reaching into my jacket pocket for my mobile phone when Dunn flung the connecting door open and startled Nina into dropping her cigarette and lighter onto the floor.

I won't repeat the names he was calling Nina and me—this is not that kind of book, after all—but he was every bit as fluent with trash talk as Nina. I didn't pay much attention to his words; I was too busy focusing on the nasty little gun clutched in his right hand.

"I ought to shoot both of you right now!" Dunn stood there, chest heaving, his handsome face contorted in rage. He waved the gun in a menacing manner, and Nina started backing up until she was standing beside me. The space between us and Dunn was a mere six feet or so. At such close range, he couldn't miss if he fired at one of us.

During the commotion, I had pressed the button on my mobile phone that would speed-dial Giles and give him the prearranged signal. Right now he should be talking to one of the policemen out in the hall, explaining just how urgent it was to get Robin Chase upstairs and into Nina's room. Help was on the way.

"Don't be ridiculous, you idiot!" Nina was screeching at Dunn. "What's the point of killing us? It's all over, Ash; it's all over!" I couldn't believe it, but she started sobbing. Amid the sobs, I could make out what she was saying, over and over: "We'd have made millions. Why? Why?"

"Wanda Harper got greedy, didn't she, Dunn? And then poor Norah Tattersall saw what you did and tried to blackmail you and Nina." I tried to introduce a note of calm into the proceedings while I was stalling, waiting for the police to arrive.

"You've got it all figured out, don't you?" Dunn sneered. "I ought to blow your head off right now." He held the gun out and prepared to shoot. I could read his intentions in his eyes; indeed, I felt them emanating from him.

This put me in an interesting dilemma, one I hadn't quite anticipated. If he did shoot me, how would I explain the fact that he didn't kill me, or at least injure me very badly?

Chapter Twenty-seven

W here the heck were Robin and his merry men?
I hadn't expected this much of a delay once
I had given Giles the signal. I couldn't believe that
all the police had left Kinsale House since I had
come to Nina's room. Surely Giles hadn't fallen
asleep, leaving me without a backup.

"Don't be an idiot, Ash," Nina was saying. "There's
no point in shooting either one of us. Don't make
it worse. One of my clients is a high-powered barrister who has never lost a murder case. I'm sure
he'll find a way to get you out of this."

"Shut up, Nina," Dunn said, making a step toward
us. "You don't know how much I'd enjoy putting a
slug in your head right about now. How stupid do
you think I am? What will it matter if I kill two
more people?"

"How stupid do we think you are?" I laughed loudly, as much to try to rattle Dunn further as to cover

up any signs of approaching rescuers. "My dear Dunn, we *know* how stupid you are. It's obvious that Wanda Harper was the brains of the operation. She even outsmarted little ol' Nina here, and that takes some doing."

Beside me I could feel Nina simmering at the boiling point. If the police didn't get here in the next minute, she was going to do something we might both regret. I could try jumping Dunn for the gun, but if it went off and a bullet struck me, I'd have some very interesting explanations to manufacture. The lack of blood would give the whole game away.

I didn't want to anger Dunn enough to provoke him into shooting, but I did want to keep him off balance if I could. "Come on, Dunn, put the gun down like a good little boy. Let Nina's barrister look after you. Nina will make sure he does a good job for you, and he probably won't even expect to be paid, after Nina gets through with him."

Dunn waved the gun in my direction again and called me one of those unimaginative names that homophobes often use, telling me to shut up. "I know Nina will screw anything in pants, but even she can't work miracles."

Two things happened then. Nina launched herself straight at Dunn, fingers curled into claws, ready to scratch his eyes out. At the same time, Robin and two of his men burst through the door from Dunn's bedroom, shouting for him to drop his gun.

Dunn dropped the gun, as much from the furious swiftness of Nina's attack as from surprise at the burst of sound behind him.

It took two of Robin's men about three minutes to subdue Nina, and by that time Dunn was begging for protection. His face was decorated with deep scratches, which were beginning to bleed profusely. After they pulled Nina off him, he went away quite happily with Robin's men.

Panting, Nina sat in a heap on the floor. Robin bent to offer her a hand, and Nina accepted it, rising to her feet in a graceful motion. "Thank you, Detective Inspector. I don't know *what* came over me, to act like that. What you must think!"

"That was rather a dangerous thing to do, Miss Yaknova," Robin said in a tone of mild reproof. "Dunn could very easily have shot you or Dr. Kirby-Jones."

From the look Robin directed at me, I suspected that he thought it would have been no more than I deserved.

"He didn't, did he, Detective Inspector Chase?" I smiled. "And now you have the murderer and can wrap the case up. All signed, sealed, and delivered."

"I suppose I should thank you, Dr. Kirby-Jones," Robin said, eyes glinting at me from over Nina's head.

"No thanks are necessary, my dear fellow," I said modestly. "I'm delighted to do what I can to assist you."

"I said only that I should thank you, Dr. Kirby-Jones, not that I would." Robin's broad smile and Nina's unladylike guffaw did not disturb me in the least.

Enter Giles from stage left, startling us all. "Simon, are you okay? What happened? I couldn't wait any longer." He had flung the door open with a bang and advanced rapidly in the room. His hand clutched my arm, and the urgency of his tone and his concern for me touched me.

"I'm just fine, Giles; no need to worry. Dunn is safely in custody now, and Detective Inspector Chase can now wrap up another case successfully."

"Good!" Giles said, letting go of my arm. "It's a good thing Simon did your work for you, Detective Inspector. There's no telling how long this might have dragged on."

Ah, jealousy! The dear boy still hadn't learned.

Robin glowered at Giles, but when he spoke he ignored him completely. "I shall of course take statements from both you and Miss Yaknova, Dr. Kirby-Jones, but first I must attend to Mr. Dunn. Perhaps in the morning, however?"

"Certainly, Detective Inspector," I said, and Nina nodded. The rush of adrenaline had subsided, and now Nina looked very tired indeed. She had much to contemplate, with one of her star authors turned into a double murderer, not to mention the fact that she had alienated several of her other prime money-earners.

Robin inclined his head politely to us before leaving the room. At some point Robin would no doubt get over his little snit that I had beaten him to the solution of another murder case. I would remind him in the morning that I had no intention of seeking any public credit for what had happened, and maybe that would put him in a better frame of mind.

"Nina, is there anything we can do for you right now?" I asked.

Nina, in the act of lighting yet another cigarette, cut her eyes up at me. "No, Simon, dear," she said, expelling smoke, "I think you've done quite enough for now." Her eyes narrowed. "Was that little deal you offered me just a ruse to get Ash to confess, or did you really mean it?"

"Why, Nina," I said, batting my eyelashes at her. "I'm devastated, simply devastated, to think that you'd consider me capable of that kind of manipulation. Why, you'd think I was just as bad as you!"

"Ha, ha, Simon," Nina said. "Very funny."

"Just remember all this, Nina," I said, turning serious. "We can continue to do business, but you're reformed, as of this moment. Got it?"

Nina nodded. "If you wouldn't mind letting the others know that you're sticking with me, Simon, there's a dear."

"I'll tell them, Nina, but it's up to them whether they choose to have anything further to do with you."

"Yes," she said, "I know. *Qué será*, and all that."

As Giles and I left her, she was reaching for the phone, perhaps to call her barrister friend on Ash's behalf.

On the way to our rooms, Giles turned to me, an indignant frown on his face. "I can't believe that you would keep that woman as your agent, Simon, after all she's done to you and to the others."

"I'm sure you've heard the adage, Giles: 'better the devil you know,' etc."

"I suppose, but aren't you taking some risks with her?"

"Perhaps." I paused in front of my bedroom door to look into his eyes. "But for now, at least, I have the upper hand, and I rather prefer that position."

"Don't I bloody know it," Giles said under his breath as he followed me into my room.

"I was beginning to think that you had fallen asleep again, Giles," I said, making myself comfortable in a chair. "It took a bit longer for the police to arrive than was strictly comfortable."

Giles's wounded look made my lips twitch into

the beginnings of a smile. "Simon! How could you think I would let you down like that? No, don't answer; I know you're just having me on!" He plopped down on my bed and scowled at me. "I got your signal and went to the copper on duty in the hall right away. But what we didn't know was that Dingleby had just reported to Chase that someone had taken a gun from the gun room."

"Ah, so that's where Dunn got it," I said. "I had wondered what he was doing with a gun."

"Because of that, it took a couple minutes to get the message to Chase, but I must say, once he heard what I had to tell him, he couldn't get upstairs quickly enough." Giles pouted at me. "He couldn't let Dunn hurt a hair on your head; that's for sure."

"Giles, dear boy, you sound almost as if you wish Dunn had shot me."

"Really, Simon, you're impossible!" Giles sat up on the bed. "Of course I didn't want him to shoot you." Then he grinned. "But if he had, I would have been quite happy to nurse you back to health."

How disappointed Giles would have been, not to mention startled, when Dunn hadn't harmed me. Perhaps at some point in time I would be ready to tell Giles the truth about just what I was. But not now. Not just yet.

With a sudden insight, however, I realized how much it would bother me if Giles, upon learning the truth, wanted nothing further to do with me.

"Thank you, Giles; I appreciate your care and concern." I kept my tone purposely light. "Now, off to bed with you. Tomorrow will no doubt be a long and tiring day, but thank goodness this is all over."

"Good night, Simon," Giles said, getting off my bed. "See you in the morning." He paused at the door of his room and blew me a kiss.

"Incorrigible," I called as he shut the door between us.

I took my last pill of the day and made ready for bed. I needed only a couple of hours' sleep; then I would get up and try to get some work done. I had a new historical novel to plot, and I might as well get going with it.

The next morning, as Kinsale House began to come to life, I rang Dingleby and requested that I might have a moment of Lady Hermione's time before she became too involved in the activities of the day. I asked also whether Isabella Veryan might join us, and Dingleby responded that he would ring me back.

In about five minutes my phone rang, and Dingleby informed me that Lady Hermione and Isabella would see me in Lady Hermione's own sitting room in fifteen minutes' time. Dingleby instructed me on how to find the sitting room, and I made my way there at the appointed time.

"Good morning, Dr. Kirby-Jones," Lady Hermione boomed at me as I entered upon her instructions.

"Good morning, Lady Hermione, Isabella," I said. The two of them were seated at a small table, sipping coffee. I glanced appreciatively around the room. This was perhaps the only chamber in all of Kinsale House that had been decorated by someone with any sense of taste. Subdued colors, no fringe or tassels, a sense of light and comfort—it was a revelation.

"Do sit down, Dr. Kirby-Jones," Lady Hermione said, her voice dropping to an almost tolerable level. "Would you care for some coffee?"

"No, thank you, Lady Hermione," I said, sitting down in a chair facing the two of them.

"What did you want to talk to us about, Simon?" Isabella spoke in a tone more friendly than I had expected.

"I thought perhaps you both might like to know what happened last night," I said.

"I have spoken already with Detective Inspector Chase," Lady Hermione said. "He was somewhat brief, however. I'm sure you might provide some of the details?"

"I'd be delighted to," I said.

They listened intently as I gave them a thorough explanation of what had happened, and how I had discovered the piece of information that had led me to the truth.

"You were gambling a bit, weren't you, Simon?" Isabella observed with a wry smile.

"A bit, Isabella," I acknowledged, "but once I realized that Dunn was a fake, I knew that he had more to lose than anyone."

"Yes," Isabella said. "Millions of pounds, to be exact." She shook her head.

"It was cleverly done," I continued. "Wanda Harper had hit upon a very attractive young man with a modest bit of writing ability, and between her and Nina, they were turning him into a hugely marketable commodity."

"And that seems to be what it's all about these days," Isabella said. "Sad, isn't it?"

"I deeply regret ever having invited that young man to Kinsale House," Lady Hermione said.

"There was no way you could have known, Hermione," Isabella said. "How could any of us? We all trusted Nina at one time, and look where that got us."

"Nina did betray us, Isabella," I said. "But I think perhaps you'll find that she's turned over a new leaf."

"About bloody time!" Lady Hermione said, and I had to smile, hearing her utter such a vulgar word.

"Simon, do you think . . ." Isabella said, "well, how much of what happened here will come out?"

"Hard to say," I responded. "Nina won't be too eager to volunteer information. It's in her best interest to keep everything as quiet as possible. The truth about Dunn and his partnership with Wanda Harper will have to come out, but I don't know about anything else. Dunn knew it all, of course, since he and Wanda Harper were in on it all, and he may sing like the proverbial bird if he gets the chance."

Lady Hermione and Isabella stared at each other, dismay apparent on their faces.

"Perhaps, if I might be so bold as to suggest," I said, "a preemptive strike might be in order?"

"That's all very well in Izzy's case, Dr. Kirby-Jones. She can leak the story of her reunion with her long-lost son to the press, and it will be quite a heart-warming story." Lady Hermione frowned, and I could sense the panic beneath her words. "But that wouldn't work in my case."

Isabella laughed, the first carefree sound I had heard from her since I had entered the room. "Hermione, my dear, the time has come to put your fears aside and let Dingleby make an honest woman of you at last. You know he's wanted to for the past year."

Lady Hermione blushed. "Ridiculous," she said. "At my age."

"Nonsense," Isabella said firmly. "He adores you, and you adore him. What else matters?"

As I left them, they were planning not only Lady Hermione's wedding but Isabella's intention of alerting the press to her new status as the mother of a fellow best-selling writer.

Isabella's final words gave me much to consider. Perhaps it was time I faced up to the truth and had a long talk with Giles.

Perhaps.

Please turn the page for an

exciting sneak peek of

the next Simon Kirby-Jones mystery

DECORATED TO DEATH

coming next month in hardcover!

Chapter One

Dead people hate housework just like everybody else.

Otherwise a vampire like me wouldn't have let a stranger have the run of Laurel Cottage twice weekly. I don't keep a coffin hidden somewhere on the premises—there's no longer any need to hide in one during the day, thanks to some lovely little pills—but I nevertheless felt a bit nervous hiring a strange person to come in to clean.

Violet Glubb seemed perfectly ordinary in most respects. Other than her unfortunate name, that is. She was reasonably attractive, if one liked the type. Women, that is. I don't, at least not in that way.

Violet had a pretty face and a fair figure and was about twenty-five or thereabouts. If she were older, she concealed it well enough behind a facade of youthful exuberance and a limited vocabulary. She also seemed very much to want the job, expressing her willingness to keep Laurel Cottage in order for the not-so-modest sum I was offering. Since any other charpersons in Snupperton Mumsley, the Bedfordshire village I now called home, had thus far neglected to express the least interest in the advertisement I had posted in the village shop-cum-post office over a week ago, the job was Violet's for the taking.

She accepted the job, shaking my hand with great vigor and smiling up at me with sparkling enthusiasm in her eyes. Evidently she loved to clean; indeed, she lived to clean, if she were to be believed. I was her second client in Snupperton Mumsley, her first being Jessamy Cholmondley-Pease, the wife of one of our local councillors. She had time for at least another one or two, however.

"You might check with Lady Prunella Blitherington at Blitherington Hall, Miss Glubb," I said. I wouldn't normally wish such a fate on anyone, but Violet Glubb seemed capable enough to face even a harridan like Lady Prunella.

She interrupted with a giggle, "Nobuddy calls me that, Mr. Kirby-Jones, just plain Vi will do."

"Ah, yes . . . Vi," I said, wincing at her high-pitched amusement, "Anyway, Lady Blitherington often seems in need of assistance at the Hall."

She giggled again. "I heard tell of her, Mr. K.-J., down at the pub. They do say she be a right battle-ax."

We both turned at the sound of a loud guffaw emanating from the doorway of the sitting room. My assistant, Giles Blitherington, stood there clutching his sides in mirth. Whether he was laughing at my new nickname or the all-too-apt description of his mother remained to be discerned.

"Giles Blitherington, may I present Miss Violet

Glubb, my new cleaner. Vi, Giles Blitherington, my assistant."

Having gained control of his amusement, Giles advanced into the room and offered his hand politely to Violet. "How do you do, Miss Glubb? It's indeed a pleasure." He offered her one of his killer smiles, and I could see Vi starting to melt right in front of him.

Giles is a handsome devil, and he knows it, but his charm is such a natural part of his character that it's effortless. He is no more interested in women than I am; he's rather more interested in Yours Truly, which he makes known as frequently as he believes he can get away with it. I have thus far resisted his blandishments, because I've no idea how he'll react when—or should I say, if—he discovers that I am one of the living dead.

I cleared my throat, and Violet turned her attention back to me. "Giles assists me with my research and writing, Violet. He keeps my work existence organized. I am counting on you to help me keep the rest of my existence clean and tidy."

She giggled again. I supposed I would eventually grow used to it, but giggling females were not high on my list of Things I Can Abide. Especially since the frequency of giggles seemed inversely proportional to IQ levels, and Violet's IQ was dropping rapidly.

"They told me down at the pub you was a writing gentleman, Mr. Kayjay. I don't read much, meself, unless it's Barbara Cartland. She writes such grand love stories, dun't she?" She sighed rapturously, remembering, I supposed, one of those grand Cartlandian tales. I tried not to shudder.

"If you like love stories, Vi," Giles said, throwing a wicked grin in my direction, "I'm sure Mr. Kayjay will give you a copy of one of his favorites by Daphne Deepwood. I've heard she writes really grand love stories, too, though I've not read them."

Violet's eyes grew big. "Really, Mr. Kayjay? That'd be a fair treat, that would."

I arched an eyebrow in Giles's direction. "Yes, Vi, I might have a spare copy in my office." Since I *am* Daphne Deepwood, and well Giles knows it, I did have more than a spare copy or two in my office. But if Barbara Cartland were Violet's idea of a grand love story, she might find one of my historical romances a bit too long and complicated for her taste. Far be it from me, however, to disdain a potential fan.

While Giles entertained Violet, I went to my office to find a copy of the latest Daphne Deepwood offering, *Passion in Peru,* which was still riding high on the best-seller list. I took great satisfaction in seeing the rows of my books upon the shelves. Daphne Deepwood had penned five books thus far, and number six was in the works. As Dorinda Darlington I had published four private-eye novels, featuring a tough female shamus. Under my own name I had published two well-received biographies of medieval queens.

One of the advantages of being dead was that I required little sleep, and I spent a lot of time writing. I was even thinking of launching a new pseudonym, under which I would write cozy English village mysteries. At the rate I was stumbling over dead bodies since settling in Snupperton Mumsley, I figured I might as well make good use of my own misadventures in sleuthing.

Violet accepted the copy of *Passion in Peru* happily, and I asked Giles to show her through Laurel Cottage. "If you need anything in the way of cleaning supplies and so on, Vi, just let Giles know. He will give you money, or purchase them himself for you. Whichever works best for you."

"Ta, Mr. Kayjay," Violet beamed at me. "I can get things at the shop on my way here, if need be. It's right on me way."

"Very well," I said. "Then we're agreed, Tuesday and Friday afternoons?"

Violet nodded. "I'll be back tomorrow, Mr. Kayjay."

"Off you go then," I said, smiling as she prepared to follow Giles around the cottage. I retreated to my office and shut the door. I was about halfway through the latest Deepwood opus and determined not to slack off, as I am occasionally wont to do during the mid-book doldrums.

I was deep into a mad chase on horseback through the Kent countryside when Giles broke through my concentration. I turned to scowl at him.

"Sorry, Simon," Giles said, backing off a bit. I can appear quite fierce without meaning to, and from the look on Giles's face, I had evidently made him a bit nervous.

"What is it, Giles?" I tried not to sound annoyed.

"I wouldn't interrupt you when you're working like that, Simon," Giles said, reproach in his voice, and I relented, giving him a brief, conciliatory smile, "but you did say to remind you about getting ready for the big event this afternoon."

"What?" I frowned, trying to recall the event to which he referred.

Giles shook his head. "Honestly, Simon, if I weren't here to keep you organized, what would you do?" He approached my desk, pushed my desk calendar toward me, and pointed. I peered at it.

"Lady B. Tea. Harwood etc." I read that aloud, then groaned.

"Yes, Simon, I know. I know you detest tea at the manor, but this ought to be interesting." Giles laughed in wicked glee. "Remember who the guest of honor is?"

Comprehension dawned, as my brain finally cleared of Kentish fog. "Ah, yes, the King of Home Decorating. Hezekiah Call-Me-Zeke Harwood." I laughed. "Or should I say the Queen of Home Decorating?"

"The one and only," Giles said, smiling. "And given the bitchy comments you've made about him, surely you wouldn't want to miss a minute of the festivities."

"No," I said, standing up and stretching. Even my neck and shoulders get cramped from hunching too long over a computer screen. "I imagine he's even more outrageous in person than he is on television. And some of the travesties he's wreaked upon those poor folk who've agreed to let him redecorate their homes for his program!"

Laughing, Giles said, "Then we'll expect you at Blitherington Hall in about an hour. I'm off to see whether Mummy needs help with any last-minute arrangements."

"I'll be there," I replied, gazing at my computer screen. There was something about that chase scene that wasn't quite right. Perhaps just a few more minutes.

"No, Simon," Giles said. "Save the file, and turn it off. If you sit back down there, we'll never see you. And Mummy would be *so* disappointed if you're not there."

Relieved would be more like it, I thought. Giles's mother and I had an uneasy relationship. She resented my giving him a job, which she considered beneath his dignity as "Sir" Giles, Lord of the Manor, and she also feared I had designs on what remained of his virtue. If she only knew that it was he who had designs on mine, the poor dear would no doubt faint dead away.

"Right you are, Giles," I said, sighing. I'd leave Marianna and Charles dashing along through Kent for a while yet. They would keep.

I followed Giles to the front door. "Do you think Violet will work out?"

Giles paused in the act of pulling on his jacket. He grinned. "She's taken quite a shine to you, Simon. All the while I was showing her around the cottage, she kept talking about how distinguished and handsome you are, Mr. Kayjay." He mimicked her voice and her giggle so well I couldn't suppress a shudder of distaste.

"I could always tell her, Simon, that you're spoken for. And by whom."

He never lets up, and it wouldn't do to let him realize that I've begun to weaken, ever so slightly. I gave him The Look, as he called it. The one that was supposed to quell him, but which had begun to lose its effect lately.

"Well, then, Simon, I'll be off. See you in a while." Not cowed in the least, he winked before opening the door and heading for his car. I watched him walk away, enjoying the view, then shut the door and leaned back against it.

All I needed was a moonstruck cleaning lady *and* Giles competing for my romantic attentions. Times like this I almost wished I did have a coffin to which to retire during the day. So much for the old days, I thought, as I headed upstairs for one of the magic little pills that makes my existence as a vampire free of the need for blood.

Trusting that I had timed it right, I arrived at Blitherington Hall some two hours after Giles had left Laurel Cottage. Figuring that a television celebrity of the magnitude of Zeke Harwood would not deign to arrive on time, I had lingered at home, jotting down notes for the village mystery I was contemplating writing. By the time I arrived there were several cars in the forecourt of the Hall, and I parked the Jaguar behind the tatty Golf belonging to the vicar and his wife.

Giles had managed to talk his mother out of a garden party, with the whole village in attendance, persuading her that a more intimate tea would be the proper event with which to welcome a television celebrity and his entourage. Not to mention that it was far less expensive. I was thankful not to have to bring along sunglasses and a hat to ward off the sun, made necessary by attendance at an outdoor function. Those pills I take make it possible for me to go about in the daytime, as long as I take sensible precautions against the sun. But it's much easier in the fall, when the sun heads down quite soon in the afternoon. The brisk temperature outside is quite refreshing; to me, at least. I think I might have enjoyed the garden party more. At least there would have been more people between me and dear Lady Prunella.

I clanged the ornate door knocker up and down a few times and waited. Finally the door opened, and I stepped inside.

"Good evening, Thompson," I said. "How are you this evening?"

"Tolerable, Professor, tolerable," the venerable butler responded in his raspy voice. A rather unprepossessing specimen, and eighty if he was a day, Thompson wavered on thin legs, blinking at me. He should have been retired long ago, but Lady Prunella was far too cheap to pension him off. She could never afford to replace him, because no one in his right mind would have worked for her the past thirty-five years with the devotion that Thompson had displayed.

"If you'll follow me, sir," Thompson said, tottering off in the direction of the drawing room.

"You needn't announce me, Thompson," I said, halting him before he had gone more than a few steps. I hated to see the poor old thing run back and forth like this, when he ought to be resting somewhere with his feet up and a nice tot of whiskey at hand for relaxation.

Thompson stopped and turned around. "As you wish, Professor. I'm sure you know the way."

"Certainly, Thompson." I smiled at him, and his lips twitched in response. He lurched back toward the front door to await the next arrival, and I strode on to the drawing room.

The buzz of several conversations assailed me as I opened the door. There were about fifteen people in the room, including Giles and Lady Prunella, one of our local councillors and his wife, and the vicar and his good lady. Lady Prunella was engrossed in delivering some sort of mini-tirade to the councillor and thus too busy to notice me, and I sidled up to the vicar, Neville Butler-Melville, and his wife, Letty, who stood sipping their tea on the side of the room well away from our hostess.

They welcomed me with warm smiles. I had worried, after the nasty murder which occurred right after I had settled in Snupperton Mumsley, that they would rather have nothing further to do with me.[*] Fortunately they held nothing against me, and we had become much better acquainted since then.

"What a lovely hat, Letty," I lied. Poor Letty hadn't the fashion sense God gave a duck, but she did try, however misguided her efforts. I figured I might as well encourage her. Neville was so devoted to her, he never realized how ridiculous she looked. The concoction of feathers and fruit she sported atop her head looked like parakeets having an orgy in the produce section, but it was colorful, if nothing else.

Letty flushed with pleasure, and Neville beamed with pride. Neville was scrumptious in his clerical kit, as ever the handsome poster boy for the Anglican Church.

"How's the latest book going, Simon?" Neville asked. "Didn't you tell me you were working on a study of medieval queenship?"

"Yes, Neville, that's right, and it's going well, if slowly." Only Giles among the locals knew that I wrote popular fiction, and I was working on a scholarly book, in between stints on romances and mysteries. At the rate I was going, the scholarly book wouldn't be finished for another two years, at least.

Before Neville could launch into a series of tedious questions—he fancied himself as quite the amateur historian—I changed the subject with ruthless speed. "Isn't it exciting to think of our having such a celebrity in our midst for the next week?"

"Oh, yes, Simon," Letty replied with great enthusiasm. "I shouldn't confess to indulging in something so frivolous, but I do so enjoy watching Mr.

---

[*] Author's note: Kindly consult *Posted to Death* for further details.

Harwood's program, *Très Zeke*. Such a clever name, don't you think? I've taken some of his ideas and adapted them for use in doing some redecorating at the vicarage. And with, though I say it myself, quite lovely results."

As Neville beamed approvingly upon his wife, I kept a polite smile plastered on my face. I had seen Letty's "adaptations," and they were no more successful than Letty's attempts to dress herself with some sense of style or taste.

"Of course," Letty continued a bit wistfully, "if one had the budget most of Mr. Harwood's clients seem to possess, it would all go so much more easily, I'm sure."

"No doubt," I said. Most of the persons who appeared on Harwood's program were already well heeled, or they couldn't have afforded the hideously extravagant paints and fabrics that Harwood never failed to choose for his work. The program footed half the cost of the redecorating, but it was still an expensive proposition for those lucky enough to be chosen for the program. "I wonder when the man of the hour will deign to appear?"

Before either Neville or Letty could reply to the sarcasm-laden question, a hush fell over the room. We turned to see what had occasioned the quiet.

A few steps inside the doorway, accompanied by four people, there stood a man of average height, going bald at the front, dressed in a purple suit with a pink shirt. Ignoring the people awaiting him, he surveyed the room, his lip curling upward in disgust.

"What a dump."